High Courage

A   Keep
B   Inner Ward or Bailey.
C   Outer Ward or Bailey.
D   Kitchens and other outbuildings.
E   Chapel.
F   Curtain walls.
G   Drawbridge.
H   Moat.
J   Stabling (thatched) & servant quarters.

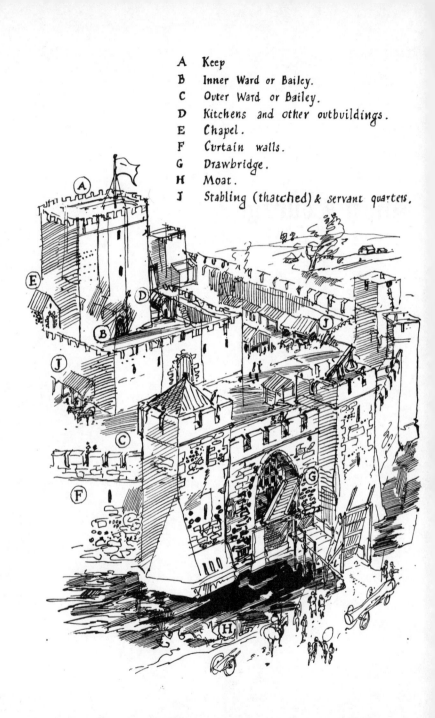

High Courage

by Rosemary Weir

illustrated by Ian Ribbons

Farrar, Straus & Giroux • New York
An Ariel Book

Copyright © 1967 by Rosemary Weir
First American printing, 1967
Library of Congress catalog card number: 67–19881

Printed in the United States of America

Designed by Marion Hess

Contents

High Courage

1

The Castle Falls

It was the noise that was so terrible. Richard knew that as long as he lived he would never be able to forget the dreadful sounds which came to him through the narrow windows in the high stone tower.

First, there was the wind, howling and screaming around the castle walls, and the rain, flinging itself from the leaden sky in solid sheets, as a man flings water from a bucket to cleanse a stable floor. And above these sounds came others more sinister: the shouts of angry men, the alarmed neighing of horses, the twang of the bow and hiss of the arrow as it sped through the air, and above all the steady, relentless blows of a battering ram against the castle gates.

"Come away from the window, my son," said Richard's mother faintly, and he turned obediently and went toward the great bed where she lay with her week-old daughter in the crook of her arm.

"I should be down there at my father's side!" said Richard in a choked voice. "Not here, sheltering with women and babes."

His mother stretched out a hand and clutched him by his arm.

"You are not yet twelve years old," she said. "There is time

enough for you to play the man. Besides, your father
ordered you to stay and bear me company. Would you have
me, weak as I am, endure this horror alone?"

"You have your women," said Richard, and his voice
sounded cross because of his anxiety. "Where are they?"

"Weeping and praying in their own chamber," said his
mother. "Joanna is half out of her mind with fear and I bade
Petronilla take her away. Fear is contagious and we have
need to keep our courage high."

"Mother—" Richard hesitated, his fingers playing nervously with the fringe of the bedcover. "Mother, if they
should succeed in breaking through, what will they do to us?
Will they—" his voice faltered and he went on in a whisper—"will they—kill us?"

The woman in the great bed lay very still. She neither
moved nor spoke until the baby stirred suddenly and gave a
little cry. She gathered the tiny bundle closer into the
protection of her arms and tried to smile, although her face
was as white as the bleached linen bed curtains around her.

"Kill us? Why, Richard, what are you dreaming of? My
Lord of Banworth may be against the King but that does not
make him a savage. He does not wage war on women and
children."

"*He* may not, but his men—" Richard's voice sank again to
a whisper. "I have heard tales—"

"Tales told to frighten children when they are naughty,"
said his mother. "It is your nurse who has told you these
dreadful tales, is it not?"

"Yes, it was Joanna," admitted Richard. "I wish you would
not call her my nurse, Mother. I am too old for nurses."

"In noble families a boy may well keep his nurse until he
is almost a man," his mother reminded him. "If she does

naught else than care for his clothes, she still reckons herself to be his nurse."

"Well, we are not so noble as all that," retorted Richard, and was rewarded by seeing an amused smile spread over his mother's face.

"Do not say that to poor Joanna," she said. "She takes great pride in being a servant in the household of one of England's oldest families, even though our home is not grand as the Baron Banworth's new castle. A great, horrid monstrosity it is, from all I hear, with newfangled rounded towers and window glass in the Great Hall. Money cannot buy good taste, my son, and my Lord of Banworth is of the new rich. He owes all he has to Simon de Montfort, the Earl of Leicester." She glanced at Richard's face as she spoke and, seeing the lines of strain relaxing a little as his mind was diverted, she made a great effort to go on.

"Odo the minstrel, who recently visited Banworth Castle, told me that in all things the Baron and his wife love to make a rich show. They are pretentious, and are bringing up their son to imagine himself only a little less than Prince Edward himself. The boy has his own greyhounds and falcons, his own dog-boy, and a body servant as well as his nurse. The minstrel said that the boy has a cloak lined with miniver, but this I cannot believe, for who would trust a boy with such riches? More like, it is of vair. The result of all this indulgence is that the boy is spoiled and overbearing, as one would expect."

"I care not for rare furs," said Richard, "but I envy him his hounds. Father says—" he stopped speaking abruptly as the din outside rose to a climax and burst into a great explosion of sound. Men yelled, steel clashed on steel, and with one final crash the gates of the outer bailey fell under the

battering ram's crushing blows. A triumphant yell went up
from the enemy, and Richard, peering through the window
slit, saw with horror the Baron's men swarming across the
drawbridge and into the bailey, driving his father's forces
before them. He groaned as he watched men he had known
all his life falling before the overwhelming numbers of the
enemy, their swords dropping from their lifeless hands.
Then, into the thick of the desperate battle rode the Earl of
Travers. He was mounted on his huge black war horse,
heavy with the accouterments of war. Man and beast were
so encased in armor that they looked like a centaur forged in
steel. Even in the midst of his terror Richard felt a warm
thrill of pride. Like a statue, the Earl sat his horse until a
surge of enemy soldiers surrounded him, and when they
dispersed, the saddle was empty and the great horse stood
alone.

Richard gave an inarticulate cry. His legs felt weak and he
staggered, groping with his hands to steady himself against
the wall.

"What is it?" cried his mother. "Richard, what is happen-
ing? What have you seen?" As she spoke, she raised herself
in the bed and the baby woke and began to cry lustily. The
door was flung open, and two women, distraught with terror,
rushed into the room.

"Oh, m'lady, m'lady! M'lord is taken! He is dead for sure!"

"We are lost! The enemy are within the walls! What is to
become of us? What shall we do?"

Richard's mother spoke quietly and sternly.

"Be silent, both of you, nothing is to be gained by lack of
control. Richard, what saw you from the window? Is—is it
true your father is taken?"

"They—they dragged him from Pompey's back," Richard

stammered. "A whole crowd of men—his sword was broken in two. He—he—"

Suddenly he could bear it no longer. He could no longer stay cowering in an upper chamber in company with a sick woman and weeping servants, he, a scion of the House of Travers, while his father was in mortal danger below. Before either of the women could stop him, he fled through the door and raced headlong down the stone stairs until he reached the Great Hall, deserted except for old blind Odo and the small, wizen-faced boy who was his guide. Snatching a short-sword from its place on the wall, he ran on, out into the cold, steely rain, out into the midst of the enemy hordes. The gale rose to a scream as he battled against its force, and he screamed himself, although he was unconscious of making any sound.

"My father! My father!" he shouted, and lunged with his sword at the first burly figure which blocked his path.

The blade glanced harmlessly off the man's thick leather jerkin, and then his wrist was caught and held in a grip of iron while a rough voice said: "Why, you murderous little runt! Would you run me through like a fowl on the spit?" His grip tightened until Richard, in agony, dropped his sword to the ground. Red lips grinned at him out of a dark, hairy face. Hard gray eyes stared at him reflectively and then creased in a sardonic smile.

"Who may you be? Who's your father?"

"My father is the Earl of Travers!" cried Richard proudly, and regretted the words as soon as they were spoken. Why, oh, why had he not had the wit to say he was one of the stable boys? No one would bother with such small fry, but the Earl's son would be a rich prize for this soldier to take before his lord.

The black-bearded man gave another cruel twist to Richard's arm so that he turned faint with pain. For a moment the world swam around him, the din died away to a murmur, and he began to slide to the ground.

"Here—hold up, runt!" exclaimed his enemy. "What ails you? Would you swoon like a woman at the first touch of pain?" He let go so abruptly that Richard fell in a heap on the ground. The mud, churned up by hundreds of scuffling feet, spattered him, soaking right through his tunic until he felt it cold against his skin. But the chill revived him and suddenly all fear went and his temper rose. Was he, Richard Travers, to lie like a dog at the feet of his enemy? He felt for the sword and jumping up drove it with all his strength against the big man's ribs. Again the stout leather jerkin deflected the blade, but the blow had caught him off-balance and he fell, in his turn sprawling in the mud. Richard leaped over his thrashing body and fled. In and out of the crowd he went, dodging horses' hooves, slipping between fighting men, in constant danger of being struck down by sword or arrow. Some of his father's men had retreated into the keep and were firing wildly and indiscriminately into the melee through the arrow slits in the thick stone walls. In the hand-to-hand fighting, it was impossible to distinguish friend from foe.

Still, Richard ran on, his breath coming in deep sobs as he ran. He had no plan; he was caught up in the nightmare of war, and horror possessed his whole being. Blood ran down his face from a gash on his forehead he had no memory of receiving, his cold hand still clasped the short-sword, his eyes were wide and fixed, and for a time he was as stupid with terror as a mouse under the harrow. He found a corner between the chapel and the farriery, an oasis of quiet in the midst of battle, and slid into it, leaning with his back against

the rough stones of the chapel wall. Water poured down on him from the thatched roof, and the noise of fighting surged around him like the roar of the sea, but here, in his sanctuary, he could rest for a moment, recover himself, and take stock.

The castle had fallen to the enemy; this he must painfully accept. His father had been dragged from his horse and was, at best, a prisoner, at worst—dead. His mother lay helplessly in her bower with the new little sister by her side. His father's men were still fighting bravely but were outnumbered, at least three to one. Soon, my Lord of Banworth would sit, victorious, in the Great Hall, and after that— what?

Richard set his teeth. He knew very well how the victors sometimes behaved in this most cruel civil war, when baron warred with baron and the supporters of that upstart foreigner Simon de Montfort, Earl of Leicester, battled with the nobles who remained loyal to their king. There were many loyalists, Earl Travers among them, who admitted to themselves the imperfections of that king, but the fact remained that he was their sovereign lord, Henry III, and they owed him fealty.

When the trouble started, Richard's father had openly declared himself to be for the King. This action had taken courage, for his own small castle was situated dangerously close to the lands held by the rival faction, and in particular to that newest and most up-to-date fortress in the land, the castle of my Lord of Banworth, a baron as new as his castle, but rich and powerful. Trouble had to be expected from this quarter and trouble came swiftly, for word had soon reached Lord Travers that my Lord of Banworth was on the march with a great company of knights and other fighting men. Preparations were at once put in hand to withstand a siege; cattle were driven in from the surrounding farmlands, every building within the outer walls was stacked high with provisions for man and beast, swords were sharpened on the grindstone, and every man saw to his bow and fashioned arrows by the score. Then the great gates were shut and fastened, and as the strong iron bars clanged into their sockets, every soul within the castle sent up a prayer that they would hold the hostile forces at bay.

On the fifth of October, in the year of the Lord 1264, Richard, looking from a window of an upper chamber, saw a cloud of dust on the horizon, and out of the cloud came a horseman approaching the castle at full gallop. He watched uneasily as the man clattered over the drawbridge, was admitted by the guard, and disappeared into the keep. Richard raced downstairs and into the Great Hall, where his father was holding council with his knights.

In his mind's eye Richard re-created the scene: his father sitting before the flaming logs on the hearth, his men grouped around him, silent and uneasy, their hounds stretched on the rushes at their feet, the flickering firelight playing on the rough stone walls, hung here and there with painted canvas depicting hunting scenes in bright colors. On the dais at the far end of the hall, servants set up a trestle table for the evening meal, covering it with a linen cloth, drinking vessels, salt cellars, and the large rounds of bread which served each man as a plate on which to put his meat. Good smells of cooking wafted in from the kitchen buildings near at hand, the smell of roasting pork and venison which made Richard hungry in spite of his anxiety to hear what news the messenger had brought. The smell of food mingled with the smell of the Great Hall itself, woodsmoke and strewing herbs and wet dogs. It was a homey odor which Richard had known ever since, as a baby, he had lain in the carved wooden cradle before the hearth fire, rocked gently by every passer-by. The whole scene was familiar and dearly loved, but it all ended on that dreadful evening when the horseman came riding so urgently with news of an enemy on the march.

After that had come bustle and confusion, and out of the confusion a new way of daily life, the life of a household under siege. My Lord of Banworth surrounded the castle with his vastly superior forces and his modern equipment of war, and after that it was only a question of time before the inevitable end. During these dreadful days Richard's little sister was born, and her coming seemed to carve deeper the lines on the Earl's face, grim and set though it had been before.

Food grew short; all the cattle were slaughtered, then the horses, until nothing remained in the stables but the Earl's great war horse, Pompey, and Richard's own palfrey, Starlight. Little rain fell, so that the level in the castle wells went down and down. A great silence fell over the castle then, the silence of despair. Every man in the beleaguered fortress knew that the end was near.

Now that end had come. The enemy was in possession of the castle; my Lord of Banworth, thought Richard bitterly, was probably at that moment in the Great Hall, warming himself at the hearth fire. His men were everywhere, killing and looting, while the castle's own lord, Richard's father, was—where? Dead or alive? Perhaps only his enemies knew, and the chances were they would not tell.

Richard's heart gave a lurch. His mother! What of his mother and the baby sister who lay by her side? He must return to his mother, he must! He had been wrong to leave her, for if he died defending her it would be well done. It was what his father would have him do.

He peered cautiously around the corner of the chapel. It was quiet now in the bailey, ominously quiet. The fighting was over and men went silently about the work of clearing up the debris of battle. A group of Earl Travers's men, all known to Richard, were grouped together, sullen and disarmed, guarded by soldiers with pikes. Wounded men, their groans very terrible to hear, were being carried on makeshift stretchers into the keep. The dead lay where they had fallen, victor and vanquished alike lashed by the pitiless rain. Arrows lay everywhere, their metal tips gleaming in the wet.

From the stables Starlight screamed shrilly and drummed with his hooves against the wooden walls, panicked by the smell of blood.

Cautiously, Richard crept around the chapel and, heart in mouth, darted a few yards to the shelter of the next building. This was the game larder, and beyond it stood the kitchens and from there it was only a short dash to a small door in the East Tower where a spiral staircase led directly to his mother's bower on the floor above. It was, Richard reflected grimly, like some nightmare game of hide-and-seek.

The kitchens were built close to the outerwall, a long, low thatched building of wood. Between the building and the wall was a passageway where rubbish was thrown by the scullions and lay in a festering heap. Pigs rootled there and flies buzzed, until the stench became so bad that the master cook sent boys to clean up the mess. No pigs rootled there now, they had all been eaten long ago. Richard picked his way through the refuse and came out at the farther end, within twelve feet of the door into the tower.

All seemed quiet. The body of a man in full accouterment lay face downward in the mud. He showed no signs of life. The sound of tramping feet came faintly from the other side of the building and a voice spoke curtly, giving orders Richard could not hear. The feet died away in the distance; now was the moment to gain the tower! Richard had no clear idea of what he should do to protect his mother. He only knew that with his father gone his place was at her side.

Leaving the shelter of the kitchen block, he ran, and heaved a sigh of relief as, half blinded by the rain, he gained the shelter of the tower. He raised his hands to push the wet hair off his face and then stopped, transfixed. A pikeman

stood on guard at the foot of the stairs, and as Richard stared, white-faced, the man stretched out a hand and gripped him by the arm.

"Not so fast," he said. "What business have you here?"

"I wish to rejoin my mother," said Richard desperately. "Let me pass."

The man bent down and looked more closely at the bedraggled little figure before him. Under the mud he could discern the fine cloth of which the clothing was made and catch the glitter of the brooch at his throat. He smiled, a slow, triumphant smile.

"So!" he said. "Having accounted for the old dog, we now have the whelp! Come with me, whelp. My Lord of Banworth will welcome your company in the Great Hall."

2

In the Hands of the Enemy

As Richard, propelled by the iron grip of his captor, entered
the Great Hall, a desperate misery swept over him. He felt
he would rather be lying dead out there in the mud of the
bailey among the bodies of his friends than alive and well in
captivity.

Dusk was falling, and the high, vaulted hall was full of
shadows, for the torches had not yet been lit. The huge fire,
however, sent forth a ruddy glow and in its light Richard
saw the Baron, sitting at ease in the high-backed chair
which belonged to the Earl of Travers and in which no one
else had ever presumed to sit. The Baron lolled at ease, his
legs stretched out to the fire, his wet clothes steaming in the
heat of the flames. He was a red man, Richard noted with
distaste, red as a fox. His coarse, wiry hair was red, he wore
a small red beard, and his cheeks and nose seemed to reflect
the same ruddy tint. Even his eyes, as he turned his head to
look at Richard, glowed red with the reflection of the flames.

He had been divested of his armor and wore a tunic of
Lincoln scarlet fastened at the neck by a costly jeweled
brooch. Around his waist was an elaborate belt fastened by a
metal clasp, curiously wrought, such as only the wealthy

could afford. His long hose were blue and made of the finest russet. Altogether he had the air of a man of wealth and fashion, even though he had just fought a battle. Through his apprehension and misery, Richard felt a reluctant admiration. This man cut a finer figure than any who had yet come into his simple, unsophisticated life.

Around the Baron stood his knights, some still in full armor, save for their helmets, others in their hauberks of chain mail and their mail stockings and shoes. Every man held a wine cup in his hand, and it was easy to judge from the loudness of their voices and the heightened color in their cheeks that their victory had been well and truly toasted in the vanquished Earl's wine.

As Richard entered the hall with his captor, silence fell on the company, and for a brief moment every eye was on him, while no one spoke or moved. Then the red Baron shifted to greater ease in his chair, frowned, and said: "Well, what have you there? Why break in on my rest to bring me a lad who, from his looks, hails from stable or kitchen?"

"He is too small for a catch, throw him back," joked one of the knights, and during the laughter that followed, Richard's captor shifted uneasily.

"If it please you, m'lord," he said. "I do not think this is a stable lad. I caught him trying to make his way up the stairs to the Countess's chamber, which I had been bidden to guard. I questioned him and he admitted to being her son. Therefore I thought it right to bring him to you."

"I did not know there was a son," said the Baron, looking with more attention at Richard. "Bring him here to me. So, you are my enemy's son? Are there more of you? Is there a nest of young rats within these castle walls?"

Richard's temper rose, his anger was so hot that momentarily it drove out fear. He stared the Baron boldly in the eye.

"I am Richard Travers," he said. "And the only rats within these walls are those who swarmed over the drawbridge at your heels!"

A stir went through the company like a breath of wind through wheat. The Baron's thick red eyebrows drew together in a frown. He looked incredulously at Richard as if unable to believe his ears.

"Now they will kill me," thought Richard, but nothing any longer seemed real. The whole world began to waver and dissolve, voices sounded now loud, now very far away. A sweat broke out on his forehead and acute nausea rose in his throat. Then everything went silent and black as he slid to the floor in a faint.

He came to his senses with the dim realization that he was being lifted into a man's arms. He smelled the strong odor of leather and wet wool, and then the heat of the fire played on him and he knew a moment of desperate panic. Could his enemy be about to cast him into the flames? He had heard fearful stories from his father's men of what was sometimes the fate of a vanquished foe. He struggled feebly, and a voice said: "The lad is reviving. What shall I do with him, m'lord?"

"Lay him on that bench and see to the wound on his head," came the Baron's voice. "Throw a cloak over him, someone, the boy is wet to the skin. He is a bold lad, a lad one could be proud to own as a son. I wish him no ill. This war is not fought against children."

Richard felt himself set down on a bench near the fire. A heavy, fur-lined cloak was thrown over him, and a bundle of something soft thrust under his head. An arm raised him up, and he opened his eyes to see a wine cup held to his lips. He drank, and strength came flooding back. He tried to get up, but the man who held the cup pushed him gently down again and said: "Lie still, while I attend to the cut on your head."

"I—I—did not know I had one," Richard muttered, and the man smiled.

"So it always is in the heat of battle," he said. "For a time, pain is held at bay. Nevertheless, you have an ugly wound and the blood is matted into your hair."

"Wash it with wine," advised another voice. "Wine is a powerful specific against the festering of wounds."

"Warm water does as well if it be clean," said the first voice briefly, and Richard was aware of a cloth being applied to his head. The cut smarted painfully and trickles ran down his face so that he tasted the salt tang of blood on his lips. In spite of his distress, he felt pride in having received a wound in battle. It made him feel a man among men. Gradually his fear receded under the kindly treatment he was receiving, and, the bathing over, he ventured to raise himself on one elbow and look into the face of the man who tended him. He saw a brown, wrinkled face under a shock of gray hair. Blue eyes regarded him appraisingly, and the thin, rather severe mouth relaxed in a smile.

"Restored now, my small enemy?" inquired the man. "Your wound, though no doubt painful, is not deep. How came you to receive it? You should have been with your mother, not imperiling yourself in the thick of the fight."

"I was with my mother," confided Richard. "She is confined to her bed, for my new little sister is only a few days old. But from the window I saw my father fall—oh, please, tell me—is my father—dead?"

The gray-haired man did not reply. Instead, he turned

to the Baron and said: "M'lord, the boy is recovered. He begs for news of his father."

The Baron turned his head and stared at Richard without speaking. He held out his cup and a man hurried forward to refill it with wine. Still no one spoke and the silence was more terrible than tidings of bad news.

Richard's nerve snapped.

"My father!" he shouted, and his voice sounded high and shrill in his own ears. "What of my father? I saw him dragged from his horse—"

"Take him away," said the Baron harshly. "Am I to be troubled with a screaming brat? Take him, and keep him under guard."

"Come," said the gray-haired man, and bending over Richard, he whispered urgently, "Be silent, if you know what is for your own good." He helped him up and with a steadying hand on his shoulder hurried him toward the door, but Richard shrugged him off and, crossing the hall, stood at the Baron's side.

"M'lord," he said, and his voice was as steady as he could make it. "M'lord, I demand news of my father. You shall not deny me this!"

A gasp went up from the men in the Great Hall, and the Baron's face took on a darker red. His lips grew thin and tight and he slammed down his wine cup on the stool beside him with a bang that echoed through the silenced room. Then, gradually, as he glared at the small, determined figure before him, his expression relaxed, and he burst into a loud, bellowing laugh. Around him, the knights joined in his laughter uneasily, wondering what was to come next. Only Richard's face remained stern and set, and the sight of it made the Baron laugh the more.

Finally, wiping his streaming eyes on the sleeve of his

tunic, he said: "Never have I been so treated since m'lady's lap dog bit me on the thumb! It is ever the small ones that are the fiercest. This is a boy of spirit, and spirit is of all qualities the one I most admire." Then he muttered, so low that only Richard caught the words, "Would that my own son had half his pluck."

"Come!" said the gray-haired man urgently. He seemed anxious to get Richard away before the Baron's mood should change, but the huge red man put out a hand and gripped Richard by the arm.

"We have captured a tiger cub," he said indulgently. "I have a notion to take the cub home with me to be a companion for Louis, my son. They are much of an age and can study together. It will be good for Louis to have a manly lad to keep him company. He is too much with his mother and her women and it makes him soft."

"I won't go! I won't!" cried Richard, and the Baron's brows drew together again in a frown.

"You are a prisoner of war," he said with a quietness that was more unnerving than a shout. "Your father's domain has fallen to me, his men are captives, and your father—" He stopped abruptly, and Richard waited with beating heart to hear of his father's fate, but the Baron told him no more.

Turning to the gray-haired man, he said: "Sir Hugo, I commend this boy to your care. Take him away, treat him well, but keep him safe. He is to see no one, no one at all. Tomorrow he rides with us when we return home."

Richard opened his mouth to protest, but Sir Hugo hastily clapped his hand over it and hurried him out of the room.

"Be silent," he said urgently in Richard's ear. "You can do nothing but submit. Anger the Baron and you may meet with a worse fate than becoming companion to his son.

M'lord admires courage, but importunity angers him, and he would punish insolence with death. Submit patiently, and you will come to no harm."

"What will happen to my mother?" asked Richard, and his heart pounded unbearably as he waited for the reply.

"No harm will come to her," Sir Hugo assured him, and Richard felt he could trust his words. "She will remain here with her own women about her. M'lord intends to leave a small force behind to man the castle and hold it for the Earl of Leicester, but they will cause her no distress. One day, when this cruel war is over and right has prevailed, you may be able to return, but as to that, I must not predict. The future is ever hidden from our sight."

"Sir Hugo," stammered Richard, fighting down waves of panic which threatened to overcome him, "please tell me the truth. Is my father dead? I saw him fall from Pompey's back—"

"I, too, saw him fall," said Sir Hugo soberly. "But then the men closed in around him, there was hand-to-hand fighting, and when the ground cleared I saw no sign of him and I have heard naught of him since. There seems to be a conspiracy of silence about his fate and I am not in m'lord's confidence in this matter." He spoke with some bitterness, and Richard guessed that this aging knight was hurt by his lord's lack of trust. "It may be that your father was killed, or captured. It may be that in the general melee he escaped and is even now hiding within the castle walls."

"But what do you think?" cried Richard eagerly. The mere thought of the possibility of escape gave him fresh hope.

The tall, gray-haired man did not answer at once. He stared out of the doorway near which they were standing,

thoughtfully watching the men who still labored at the task of clearing the debris of battle. Rain still fell heavily on the bodies of the dead, and the groans of the wounded and dying sounded eerily through the deepening dusk. Torches were lighted, and their red smoky flare added to the unnatural horror of the scene.

At last Sir Hugo spoke.

"It would be wrong of me to raise your hopes," he said quietly. "It seems to me that a man heavily accoutered, as was your father, had scant chance of escape once he was unhorsed. Nor do I think he would attempt such an escape. This man was, by the fortunes of war, my enemy, but I knew him at court before this wretched division of loyalties began, and I knew him for a valiant man. My poor boy, I very much fear that this day's work has made you fatherless, unless—"

He paused, and Richard croaked between dry lips, "Unless—what?"

"Unless he was taken prisoner and now lies in his own dungeon," said Sir Hugo heavily. "If that is the alternative, I advise you, boy, to pray God that your father is dead."

Richard turned his thoughts painfully to the dungeons deep in the ground below the keep. His father, a merciful man and in advance of his times, never used them, but Richard and the other boys about the place had often gained a fearful thrill by venturing down the steep, worn stone steps and peering through the iron bars into the small chambers where the only light came from gratings high up in the walls and the floors oozed damp. Green slime ran down the rough stonework, and rats scuffled among the moldering straw, last remnants of some wretched prisoner's bed. In the past, Richard well knew, men had been cast into these cells and left to rot there until they died, but those men, surely, had been criminals, not honorable prisoners of war! The thought of his father in such surroundings turned him sick, and once again he swayed and would have fallen save for Sir Hugo's strong, supporting hand.

"If you are to ride with us tomorrow, you must have food and rest," said the knight. He spoke brusquely, to hide his pity for the small prisoner in his charge. Although it was the normal and accepted practice for boys of noble family to be sent during their formative years to live in the household of some other nobleman, often of superior rank, they went as friends, not as captives. They took with them their own nurse, or body servants, often their own horse and dogs. Letters reached them in the hands of messengers, giving them the news of home and bearing good wishes and affection from loving parents. Under what very different circumstances was this poor boy now being reft from his home, and what would his position be at Banworth Castle? Sir Hugo thought of young Louis, a peevish, sickly lad, alternately spoiled and bullied by his domineering, hot-tempered mother, who ruled her huge household with a rod of iron. There was little enough love and happiness at Banworth, for all the Baron's wealth.

He sighed and, stooping, picked Richard up bodily and carried him to a small room normally used as a store. A strong smell of spices came form the heavy oak chests which stood against the walls. On one of these chests Sir Hugo laid Richard down, throwing the fur-lined cloak over him, bidding him lie still and rest. Then he went out, locking the door behind him, but presently returned with food and ale and a bundle of Richard's own clothes.

"I have seen your nurse," he said. "She is half out of her mind with anxiety about you and your father. I had little comfort to give her, save that you are safe and your wound only slight. I sent word to your mother, and bade the woman pack your gear, which she at last stopped her lamenting long enough to do. Sit up, boy, you must eat and drink if you are to keep up your strength."

Richard turned his face to the wall. "I cannot," he said in a muffled voice. "I had rather die.'

"Richard," said Sir Hugo. "Richard, listen to me. When I knew your father in happier days at King Henry's court he boasted to me—who have no sons—of your courage. You were then but five years old, but already, so said m'lord Travers, you had been set on the back of his war horse and shown no fear, and you handled with confidence the most savage hound. Richard, my sons all died in infancy and I felt bitter envy of a man who could speak so of his son. Would he still feel pride in you if he could see you now? When all is against us and the future looks black, that is the time to keep our courage high."

High courage! These were the selfsame words his mother had used earlier in this fateful day. High courage, the only staff to support one when all else was bitter and black!

Richard rolled over and sat up. He took the cup and platter from Sir Hugo and ate and drank, although to swallow was an effort and his stomach revolted against the food. Still, when the meal was done, he felt better. He swung his legs off the chest without trembling, and his voice, when at last he spoke, was steady and low.

"I thank you, sir," he said. "I will endeavor to bear myself as my father would have me do."

"Spoken like a brave boy," said Sir Hugo, and smiled. "Now rest, and try to sleep, for tomorrow we ride to Banworth and you will need all your strength. The Baron has commanded me to see your mother and explain what provision he is making for her now the castle will be manned by Sir Simon de Montfort's forces. She will be confined to her own quarters, she and her babe and her women, but no harm will come to them, that I promise you. Now, what message shall I bear her from you?"

"Give her my dear love," said Richard in a choked voice. "Tell her I—I shall see her again one day."

"I will bear her your love," said Sir Hugo, and turning abruptly, he left the room, closing the heavy door behind him. Richard heard the key grate in the lock, and then there was silence, except for the far-off singing and shouting in the Great Hall as the victors celebrated their victory with the Earl of Travers's ale and wine. The scent of spices hung heavily over the small room, reminding Richard of the kitchen at feasting times when he had hung around watching the cooks prepare game pies and boars' heads and sweetmeats for the coming feast. Wretchedly he threw himself down on the chest, pillowed his head on the bundle of clothes, and covered himself with the heavy cloak. Resolutely he tried to turn his thoughts from a nightmare vision of the dungeons, and quite suddenly he passed into a deep sleep. Sir Hugo, in pity for his small captive, had placed a sleeping draft in the cup of ale. For hours Richard slept dreamlessly, to awake suddenly in the small hours with the realization that someone was scratching cautiously on the door.

3

The Departure

Richard sat bolt upright in the thick darkness, his heart thudding. Still bemused with the drug-induced sleep, he hardly knew where he was. He put out a hand to grasp the bedpost, and encountered nothing but rough stone walls. He groped for the bedcovers, and the fur-lined cloak slipped off him and fell with a soft slither to the floor. It was piercingly cold.

Again the soft scratching sound came from the door, and now Richard recovered himself sufficiently to whisper: "Who is there?"

"It is I, Odo, the minstrel," came a low hoarse voice, muffled by the thickness of the door. "Master Richard, is that you?"

"Yes, of course it is," said Richard impatiently. He jumped to the ground and felt his way over to the door. "Let me out, Odo. Quick, before someone comes!"

"I cannot," said the old blind man. "I have felt for the key but it is not in the lock. No one will come if we are quiet. They are all sleeping like the pigs they are, sodden drunk with m'lord's good wine. Master Richard, listen carefully. I can do naught to help you, but I have news which may bring comfort to your heart."

"Whisper through the keyhole," said Richard. "This door is thick and it is hard to hear."

He bent his head to the lock, and the old man's voice whispered in his ear.

"Master Richard, they know naught of m'lord your father. I heard them say so! He is not dead nor was he taken captive. It follows then that he must have made his escape."

"But that can't be so!" exclaimed Richard. "A man in full armor is helpless when he is unhorsed. I saw him myself fall from Pompey's back, and then the fight closed in—"

"When the men dispersed, your father was gone," insisted the old man. "He had vanished off the face of the earth. With my own ears I heard the knights marveling over this thing."

"I don't believe it," said Richard, but in spite of himself, hope rose in his heart. "How could such a thing be?"

"Maybe it was a miracle," whispered the old man solemnly. "The Lord is ever on the side of the righteous."

"Then where is my father now?" asked Richard skeptically. Miracles, he felt, were something which had only happened in far-off days, not in modern times, within one's own home. He was about to put more questions to the old man when the sound of heavy footfalls outside the walls of the keep startled them both into a frozen silence. When the sound died away and Richard ventured to repeat his queries, there was no response. The old man had been led silently back to his corner in the Great Hall.

Richard returned to his makeshift bed, but not to sleep. With his arms crossed under his head, he lay on his back, staring into the darkness, pondering what the old man had said.

How could his father possibly have escaped from the

enemy once he was on the ground? A man in full battle armor is helpless until he is assisted to remove his helmet and breastplate at least. The weight of the armor was prodigious, so much so that only the strongest horses could carry a man into battle. Pompey stood seventeen hands high, and his legs were like the trunks of trees. Let man and horse stay together and they were a formidable fighting unit; unhorse the man, and he was as helpless as a crab in its shell. One man he might hold at bay with his broadsword, or even two men, or three, but a rabble of men armed with pikes would have him at their mercy. Such a rabble Richard had seen with his own eyes surrounding his father when he fell. Yet, when the ground was cleared, the Earl had gone. It was impossible and yet, if Odo had heard rightly, the enemy themselves acknowledged it as a fact.

Richard's tired brain turned the mystery over and over, torn between incredulity and hope, until at last sleep overcame him once again and brought him peace.

When he again awoke, it was daylight. The winter sun streamed in through the small window with dust motes dancing in the beam. The castle seemed alive with bustle and noise. The clatter of many horses' hooves came from outside the keep, men shouted orders, cartwheels rumbled, and then followed the rhythmic tramp of marching feet. The victorious enemy was preparing to depart.

Richard jumped down from the chest. He tidied his hair with his fingers, straightened his clothing, crossed himself, and knelt down to pray. He prayed for his father, and his mother and the new little sister who were to be left alone, captives in their own home. Then he prayed for himself, that he might find courage to meet whatever the future should bring. He had scarcely finished before he heard a key in the

lock, the door swung open, and Sir Hugo came into the
room. He looked gray with tiredness, as if he had not slept,
but his face creased into an approving smile as he noted
Richard's composure.

"Tell me," he said. "The small gray palfrey in the stables,
is he by chance yours?"

"Yes, he is!" said Richard eagerly. "He's Starlight. My
father gave him to me when I reached ten years. All the
other horses have been slaughtered for food, but Starlight
was spared, he and Pompey." He paused, and asked fearfully, "Please, Sir Hugo, what has happened to Pompey?"

"He goes with us to Castle Banworth," said Sir Hugo
shortly.

"Is—is there news yet of my father?" asked Richard, his
heart beating fast.

It was as if he had not spoken. Sir Hugo's face became
blank and expressionless and he made no reply. Instead, he
picked up the heavy cloak and signed to Richard to bring his
bundle of clothes. Then, still silently, he placed a firm hand
on his shoulder and led him out of the room.

"It is true then," thought Richard to himself. "They do not
know, for if my father were captive or dead, why should Sir
Hugo not tell me?"

The Great Hall, as they passed through it, was again
deserted. The fire had died down to a pile of gray ash, wine
flagons and empty cups lay everywhere, while on the dais
the long table was strewn with the remains of a meal. Two
greyhounds crouched under the table crunching bones, and
Richard looked at them miserably. They were old dogs
whom he had known from babyhood. What would become
of them now?

He looked around for any sign of Odo, but the old man's

corner was empty and he and his boy were nowhere to be seen.

It was a relief to leave the cold, silent hall and go out into the sunshine. Overnight the whole scene had changed. The rain had cleared away and the sky was a brilliant blue. The wet ground steamed like a broiling pot under the warm rays of the sun. The bodies of the dead no longer lay in the mud like tragic, unstrung puppets. The broken swords, the discarded pikes and arrows, all were gone. Only the churned-up ground betrayed the fact that so short a time before a desperate battle had been fought within the curtain walls. Even the great wooden doors, smashed by the battering ram, had been roughly repaired and hung straight on their massive iron hinges. The portcullis was raised and the drawbridge down, ready for the departure of the Baron and his men.

Sir Hugo caught Richard's look of surprise.

"Fatigues have been at work since first light," he said. "The wounded are being cared for in the guardhouse, both friend and foe, united in the companionship of pain. Your father's villeins—such as are left of them—have been permitted to disperse to their homes. They will give us no further trouble, for they desire greatly to work on their farms. The women are calm, now they realize that we wish them no harm, and your mother, whom I have seen this morning, bears herself like the brave lady she is. These are the fortunes of war, Richard. Today you eat the bread of bitterness, tomorrow—who knows what the future will bring?"

"King Henry will overthrow his enemies!" said Richard hotly. "He reigns over us by divine right, and those who work against him are traitors to our country!"

"Bold words," said Sir Hugo dryly. "Yet there is another side to the question, and Simon de Montfort, m'lord of Leicester, seeks right and justice for an oppressed people. Soon he is to call a Parliament— But this is no time to argue politics. Look, here comes Starlight, ready for you to mount."

Richard looked eagerly across the bailey to where, outside the stables, the Baron's horsemen were preparing for the ride. Some were grooming their mounts, hissing between their teeth as they rubbed the shiny coats, others were saddling up, with a jingle of bit and stirrup iron. Boys hurried to and fro with buckets of water, horses stamped, men shouted and laughed, and the sun shone over all. In spite of his misery, Richard felt a slight lift of the heart as he saw his own small horse led toward him. It was a long, weary time since he had last ridden out. For many months the besieging forces had been encamped around the castle walls, weary, anxious months during which time they had waited, first confidently, then with waning hope, and at last despairingly for relief to come from the forces of the Crown. None came, and when the small garrison was weakened with hunger and their ammunition almost spent, the enemy had struck. Around the castle the broad acres belonging to the Earl of Travers stood untilled and unsown, for every able-bodied man among the Earl's tenants had rallied to the defense of the castle. Now, at the turn of the year, rank weeds grew where corn should have been sprouting green. There would be hunger in the land during the coming year, hunger and waste and misery, the specters, which war ever brings in its train.

Last time Richard had ridden out of the castle walls he had been at his father's side. They had spent a splendid day hunting wild boar in the oak woods which lay to the west. It was the first time his father had taken him on the chase, and now, it seemed, it was to have been the last.

"Your horse, young master," said a voice in his ear, and he came back with a start to the present. He took the reins from the man with a muttered word of thanks and swung into the saddle, blinking back his tears. Once mounted, he felt better. Starlight was his friend, dear and familiar in this nightmare of change. He leaned forward and fondled the palfrey's neck.

There was a stir among the throng of men, and Richard saw the Baron appear from the keep and stand surveying the scene. He looked enormous as he stood, legs apart, arms akimbo, with the sun turning his red hair to copper. His beard jutted out aggressively and his lips were parted in a smile. He turned to the knights surrounding him and made some jest at which they all laughed sycophantically. Then his roving gaze fell on Richard and he fell silent, thoughtfully surveying the small, sturdy boy on the little gray horse. He beckoned, and Sir Hugo said quietly, "Go to him, and mind your manners. You will do yourself no good by defiance. The Baron is not a patient man."

Richard pressed his knees into Starlight's flanks and rode forward. When he reached the spot where the Baron stood, he reined in and sat motionless, waiting.

"So!" said the Baron. "The young tiger cub rides home with us." He turned to Sir Hugo, who had crossed the bailey at Richard's side. "How does his wound? Is he fit for the ride or should he rather travel in one of the baggage carts?"

"His wound is slight, m'lord," said Sir Hugo. "The boy is fit to ride."

"Has he eaten?" demanded the Baron. "Or is he in the sulks?"

Richard's face grew red. Hot words rose to his lips, but Sir

Hugo laid a warning hand on his knee and answered quickly: "He has eaten, m'lord. He is in good fettle."

The Baron grunted. "I put him in your charge," he said. "He is to ride with you, and you shall keep his mount on a leading rein. We want no tricks."

"As you command, m'lord," said Sir Hugo quietly, and putting a hand on Starlight's bridle, he led him away.

"I don't want to be on the leading rein like a baby!" Richard expostulated when they were out of earshot of the Baron. Sir Hugo made no reply. He sent a stable lad scurrying for the extra rein and saw it attached to Starlight's bridle. Then he mounted his own horse, a great, raking black, took Starlight's rein into his hand, and rode out of the bailey in the train of the Baron and his knights. Behind them rode a company of archers, and behind them again came the tramp of feet as the pikemen, a motley rabble of men, crossed the drawbridge.

Outside the curtain wall of the castle lay the Baron's camp, where he and his men had lived for months past. Richard looked at it with interest, for so much was new to him. Every piece of equipment was of the most modern kind. The tents of the knights were rich and colorful, with the Baron's own tent more splendid than them all. Everywhere men were at work, striking camp. The great baggage wagons were loaded high with weapons and armor, sacks and barrels of food and drink, bundles of fodder and the straw-filled palliasses which served the men as beds. At the horse lines, splendid beasts were being groomed by boys little older than Richard himself. There were the draft horses that drew the baggage carts, huge, upstanding animals imported from the Low Countries, each one of great price. Here was the private army of an immensely wealthy man.

Richard, in spite of his grief, found the scene fascinating. He would have been glad to stop for a while, to look more closely at all these wonders, but the Baron and his knights rode straight on through the camp without stopping and took the road which led to the coast, with Sir Hugo and his captive bringing up the rear.

"Where is Castle Banworth?" Richard asked, as the pace slowed a little on rising ground, and he could spare the breath to talk.

"Do you not know?" asked Sir Hugo incredulously. "I should have thought that everyone in the county of Dorset would have known of Castle Banworth, since the building of it is one of the architectural wonders of our day."

"Why?" asked Richard flatly. The red Baron's new castle might be very wonderful, but he was sure it could not compare with the delights of his own dear home.

"Well, to begin with," said Sir Hugo, "it is large, the largest castle in the south of England. It is constructed on an entirely different principle from your home, Richard, being built on a level site instead of at the summit of a hill. It has two wards, one within another, and is therefore impregnable. The towers are built of rounded stones which resist the attacks of battering rams and siege engines."

"How do you know?" demanded Richard. Sir Hugo smiled.

"It has already been through its testing time at the hands of the King's troops," he said. "No device of theirs could prevail against the impregnability of the defenses. It is a fine thing the Baron has created, Richard. He had the best brains in the country and an unlimited treasure chest. Do not let your natural resentment blind you to one of the wonders of our day."

Richard was silent. Was he expected, he thought bitterly,

to take pleasure and show interest in this fine castle at which he would arrive as a prisoner? He knew he would hate it and everything about it. The Baron was a rebel and an upstart. He was against the King. His castle had been built with money supplied by the arch-traitor, Simon de Montfort. His father had said so, and his father was always right. Well, he, Richard Travers, was for the King. At this moment the House of Travers was in eclipse, but one day it would again shine forth brightly, and if the worst had happened and his father was dead, then he, Richard, would raise it to its rightful place!

The cavalcade had now reached the summit of the rising ground. The Baron drew rein to let his horse wind, and everyone else followed suit. Richard swung Starlight around, and gazed and gazed at his home, now small in the distance. Around the outer wall men still scurried like ants, but within the bailey all seemed deserted. No smoke rose from the kitchens, no flag flew from the keep. Somewhere within those walls his mother lay, with the new baby sister by her side. What must she be feeling now, alone!

Richard set his teeth. He must not weep, not in front of all these men, who were his enemies. He must convince them that a Travers could show courage in the face of grief, high courage! Sir Hugo, glancing at the small figure by his side, saw the set lips, the extreme pallor of the face, and his heart contracted with pity.

"Come," he said gently, and gathered up the leading rein as the Baron and his knights rode on down the farther side of the hill. The ground soon rose behind them, hiding Travers Castle from their sight. At the foot of the hill was open, springy downland, and the company of horsemen spurred forward, sweeping on at a gallop toward the great, new fortress by the sea.

4

Castle Banworth

Richard was very tired. Nothing would have made him admit the fact, but as the day wore on he began to wonder how much longer he could sit erect in the saddle. It had been a tiring ride, for Starlight, being so small, had kept breaking into a jog trot in order to keep up with Sir Hugo's large horse. Much of the way had been along rough roads, pitted with ruts left by wagon wheels. Whenever they could, the company of horsemen took to the grass, but in some parts of the country thick woods pressed in on either side of the road, and here the Baron and his knights rode warily, ever on the alert for sudden attack.

Now, with dusk just beginning to fall, they were in open country again and Sir Hugo, raising his head, declared he could smell the sea.

"I have never seen the sea," said Richard. "Is Castle Banworth near to it?"

"Near to it?" exclaimed Sir Hugo. "Did you not know? Castle Banworth is built upon the very cliff itself. From the south battlements you look down a sheer precipice to the sea below."

"I thought you said the castle was not built on a hill," said Richard wearily. It was an effort even to talk, but he felt that if he did not he might disgrace himself by falling asleep in the saddle and toppling to the ground.

"Nor is it on a hill," Sir Hugo told him. "From the cliff top the land stretches fair and level for miles. But the cliffs here are high and unscalable. They are nature's own fortress walls. You will love the sea, Richard. It is splendid in a storm, when the white horses, as people call the waves, batter themselves against the rocks, sending up clouds of spray. And in fair weather when the sun shines and the water is calm and blue it is the most beautiful sight in the world. Or so, at any rate, think I. You will learn manly sports at Castle Banworth, Richard, in company with Louis. You will learn to swim and sail a boat. You will learn swordsmanship and the use of the bow. You will learn to dance and play the lute, and many other courtly arts. If you are minded to pursue book learning, you may have instruction in that quarter too. The Chaplain instructs Louis, who can already read and write, and understands something of the Latin tongue."

"I have already had instruction in these things," said Richard, proudly, but truth compelled him to add lamely, "Well, in some of them at least."

"Of course you have," said Sir Hugo kindly. "But it will be more amusing for you to study in company with another boy, will it not?"

"What is Louis like?" asked Richard curiously. Sir Hugo hesitated.

"As a very little boy he was often ailing," he said. "His mother still fears for his health and is perhaps overanxious and indulgent. I should not speak like this of m'lord's son, but it is fair you should have a word of warning. Your position at Castle Banworth will be a difficult one. Do not oppose

Louis or you will antagonize Lady Eleanor, and that would be unwise."

"Why? Is she horrid?" asked Richard bluntly and Sir Hugo smiled.

" 'Horrid' is not a word to use of a lady," he said. "Let us say she is masterful. Her word at Castle Banworth is law, and she is subject to no one but the Baron himself. Watch your temper, and remember that you have ever a friend in me."

"Thank you," said Richard soberly. "Are there no other children in the castle?"

"There is little Alys," began Sir Hugo and then stopped suddenly and pointed ahead. "Look, there is the castle! Our journey is nearly at an end!"

Richard followed the pointing finger and saw, dim in the gathering dusk, the huge bulk of Castle Banworth. It looked like a whole town to him, accustomed as he was to the compactness of his own home. The outer walls stretched an immeasurable distance, tall and strong with high towers at intervals along their length. Even in the waning light and at a distance it was possible to see that the stonework was brilliantly painted in reds and blues and greens. But it was not the splendor of the castle that made Richard catch his breath in wonder, it was the sea! The last rays of the setting sun made a path of gold over the leaden gray of the great waste of waters, ruffled here and there with small white-capped waves; a ship, harbor-bound, ran before the wind with taut sail, and this was, to Richard, the final marvel, for never in all his life had he seen such speed and grace of motion.

His weariness forgotten in wonder, he rode on at Sir Hugo's side, straining his eyes for a last glimpse of the

wonderful ship. And, so, unnoticing, he crossed the drawbridge and entered the barbican, Starlight's hoofbeats sounding hollow as they rode through the great archway of stone.

The barbican, to Richard's bewildered eyes, seemed to be thronged with people. Servants held flaming torches high, and the smoky light shone on massive crenelated walls. The horses, recognizing their home and eager to return to their own stables, quickened their pace, but were checked by the grooms, who ran to their heads and led them through a farther gateway to the inner bailey, where they held them steady for the Baron and his party to dismount.

If the barbican had seemed large to Richard, the bailey seemed enormous. Numerous outbuildings clustered around the curtain walls, handsomely built and roofed with slates or lead. Smoke came from numerous chimneys, good smells of food wafted from the kitchens, a sound of chanting voices came from the chapel, while all around men and boys hurried about their work in busy, ordered confusion.

But it was the keep itself which took Richard's breath away. Never had he seen or imagined anything so splendid. Great round towers rose up into the sky, lights shone out from the narrow windows, and Richard noticed with awe that at least two of these windows were filled in with glass, a substance of which he had heard but never seen. The main doors to the Great Hall stood open, and as the Baron approached, dogs rushed out barking, among them a pair of huge, rough-coated hounds which leaped joyfully upon Sir Hugo, making a great to-do.

"What are they?" asked Richard eagerly, his shyness forgotten, for above all things he loved dogs.

"They are Irish wolfhounds," said Sir Hugo. "They were a gift to the Baron from a nobleman in that strange isle. They are the fiercest and most tenacious of hunting dogs, and worth a king's ransom. Speak to them, Richard. This one is called Shamus and the other is his lady wife, Tara."

"They are beautiful!" said Richard, and calling the hounds to him, he caressed their broad strong heads, rubbing behind their ears and stroking their hard, wiry coats. The great dogs seemed to accept him at once as a friend, and when he entered the hall at Sir Hugo's side, it was with a hand on the neck of each of the beautiful hounds. Once inside he paused, uncertain and stricken with shyness, while everyone within the hall fell silent, watching him.

The hall was as vast and as grand as everything else about the place. The great vaulted roof was filled now with the duskiness of approaching night, but the gaily decorated walls shone brilliantly in the light of numerous torches burning in cressets on the walls and in the leaping flames of the hearth fire. In front of the fire, the red Baron sat at ease in his high-backed chair, and beside him stood Lady Eleanor, the richness of her dress distinguishing her from the other ladies of the household. Near her lounged a tall, thin boy with a pasty, discontented face. He turned as Richard came in, and stared hard, then his face turned red with anger and he burst out: "Who is that boy? How dare he touch our dogs?"

At his words Lady Eleanor turned too and looked at Richard, and he, fascinated, stared back at her. She was beautiful, he thought, far more beautiful than any lady he had ever seen, but she was frightening too. Her bright blue eyes were hard and unfriendly, her beautiful mouth was set in cruel lines. She frowned, and Richard felt a cold chill pass over him and his hands tightened on the rough coats of the great hounds, seeking comfort from their friendliness.

"Who is this boy, m'lord?" Lady Eleanor demanded, turning to the Baron, and her frown deepened.

The Baron laughed, but Richard's quick ear caught an undertone of unease.

"A prisoner of war, m'lady," he said. "He is the son of the Earl of Travers and I brought him here to be a playmate for Louis."

"I want no upstart rebel for a playmate!" exclaimed Louis passionately.

Richard's temper rose. His fears and shyness forgotten, he let go the dogs and crossed the hall to confront the group around the fire.

"Rebels yourselves!" he cried, and a gasp went up from the knights and ladies who thronged the room. "You are the rebels! I am for the King!"

There was a horrified silence. The red Baron grew redder still, Lady Eleanor turned white with rage, and Louis hit out at Richard, who caught his arm and held it until Sir Hugo, who had strode after him, plucked him away and held him fast.

"You young fool," he muttered in Richard's ear. "This is a

fine start." Then, turning to the Baron, he said apologeti-
cally, "The boy is overwrought, m'lord. He asks your pardon.
He is only a little lad, and very weary after our long ride."

"Take him away," said the Baron hastily, with an uneasy
glance at his wife. "See he is rested and fed!"

Louis laughed loudly. "You speak as if he were a new
hound, Father," he said. "Take him to the kennels, Sir
Hugo."

"The head cook is asking for a new boy," put in Lady
Eleanor. "Let him go to the kitchens."

"The boy is of noble birth," said the Baron shortly. "He is
an honorable prisoner of war. He lives with us, as one of the
household, and will bear Louis company at his studies and
sports. This is my wish. Let me hear no more about it."

"Come," said Sir Hugo, and led Richard away. He took
him out of the big doors through which they had entered,
into the darkness of the inner bailey, and up an outside flight
of stairs to the floor above. Here was a small chamber
containing a bed, a chest, and a couple of wooden stools. A
fire burned in the hearth and on the floor was a small carpet
in glowing colors, such as Richard had never seen before.
The deep-set window was furnished with heavy wooden
shutters, and these Sir Hugo now closed, for it was cold in
the small room in spite of the fire.

"This is my sanctum," he said. "I am fortunate in having
such a room to myself, but I am no longer young and the
Baron is indulgent to those he loves. I am minded to keep
you in here with me, Richard. A palliasse on that chest will
serve you for a bed."

"I am very grateful to you, sir," said Richard in a low
voice.

Sir Hugo looked uneasily at the small figure standing so

disconsolately before the fire, and tried hard to think of anything comforting to say. He knew only too well that a rough time lay ahead for this little prisoner, so far from home. Lady Eleanor was a ruthless, spiteful woman, and Louis was a weak, spiteful boy. Richard would receive hard treatment at their hands. While he and the Baron remained at Castle Banworth, matters would not be so bad, but when next they rode out on de Montfort's business, as they were bound to do, then Richard's lot would be unenviable indeed.

He sighed, and sinking down wearily in the big chair, he put out a hand and drew Richard to his side.

"My small friend," he said, "be advised by me. There are times when defiance and rebellion are useless. They help no one, least of all yourself. Be patient and keep that hot temper of yours under control. In the short time you have been here you have antagonized Lady Eleanor, and she wields great power in this castle. Louis may come around. He is a lonely boy, and if you set yourself to please him, all may yet be well in that quarter. Bide your time, Richard, bide your time."

"For what?" asked Richard bitterly. Then, with sudden hope, he went on: "Do you think that soon the King's forces will prevail?"

"I did not say that," said Sir Hugo. "Nor would I wish it so. I am for Simon de Montfort, for I believe his cause to be just. This country of ours groans under great injustice, Richard. The people suffer wrongs which must and shall be righted. De Montfort seeks to hold a Parliament which shall represent the people. The King is a weakling, the puppet of unscrupulous men. You are too young to understand these matters and so, very understandably, you follow your father's lead. I say no word against your father. He was an honorable and upright man, but I believe his views to be mistaken, that is all."

Richard was silent. It was all so confusing. Until now he had never doubted but that his father was in the right and everyone who held opposing views was a traitor to England. Yet here was Sir Hugo, a brave, gentle man whom he could not but admire, holding other opinions, just as firmly as his father held his. Who was right? Was Simon de Montfort not, in fact, a monster, as he had been brought up to believe? How difficult grown-up life was, and how terrible! Because grown men could not agree, he, Richard, was now reft from his parents, his home, and all that he loved, and cast into the coldness and disdain of an alien household with no hope of escape, and no comfort except for the kindness of one man. Waves of homesickness swept over him, drowning him in misery.

At this hour, at home, they would have been sitting down to the evening meal, Richard at his father's right hand at the high table on the dais. Below them, in the body of the hall, long trestle tables would be set up for the household, every one of whom, man and woman, was an old and valued friend. Beneath their feet the dogs had lain, waiting hopefully for scraps of food. There had been warmth and light and cheerfulness as the wine went around and, perhaps, some traveling minstrel sang and played to them while they ate. After the meal, when the tables were cleared away, there had been games: wrestling and trials of strength for the men, and a romp of Hoodman's Blind for the younger people, the women, and children. When bedtime came, Richard had slept safely on a truckle bed in the upper chamber, near the great curtained bed of his parents, warm under his fur-lined coverlet, his favorite dog curled up on his feet. His mother took two little smooth-coated dogs into bed with her to keep her warm. He wondered what they would think of the new baby, and at the thought of her the tears again started into his eyes. He wiped them away hastily with the back of his hand and prayed that Sir Hugo had not seen.

Sir Hugo got up from his chair and stretched.

"Heigh-ho," he said. "I must go down and join the company below. It is time for supper, and my absence would be remarked and resented. Stay you here, Richard, and I will have food brought to you. It is best you keep out of sight until Lady Eleanor's wrath subsides. I will talk to her of you and try to bring her around to a more friendly feeling."

"I am not hungry," said Richard morosely. "Their food would choke me."

"Now that is foolishness," said Sir Hugo gently. "Good food chokes none. It is false pride that closes the throat. Stay here, and I will send a messenger such as you do not expect."

"Who?" asked Richard curiously, but Sir Hugo only smiled mysteriously and went away.

Left alone, Richard flung himself down on the carpet before the fire. He fingered the woven fabric curiously, admiring the bright colors and the curious pattern. He had heard of these floor coverings; knights who had fought in the Holy Land brought them back from far-distant lands. Sir Hugo must surely be a man of wealth, for only the wealthiest put such treasures on the floor to be trodden upon. More often they adorned the walls, safe from trampling feet. Sir Hugo was a good man. It seemed queer that he should be for that traitor, de Montfort. Could it be that what he had said was true, and that de Montfort had a righteous cause? Could it possibly be wrong to support one's sovereign lord, the

King? It was all too much for Richard's tired brain. Lying flat on the soft carpet, the warmth of the fire playing on him, he dropped into a light sleep.

He was awakened suddenly by the click of the door latch and started up in bemused alarm.

Framed in the doorway stood a little girl, smaller than Richard himself, very slight and fair. Her long hair hung loose about her shoulders, only confined by a gilt circlet around her head. She wore an overdress of blue wool over a super-tunic of yellow linen with long, light sleeves buttoned to the elbow. She looked very fine, but her small face was pale and anxious and she stared at Richard uncertainly out of her large brown eyes. In her hands she held a platter of food, but in spite of this it was obvious that she was no serving maid.

"Why—who are you?" asked Richard. She smiled at him shyly, holding out the food.

"I am Alys," she said.

5

Alys

For a moment the two children looked at each other in silence, then Alys crossed the room and put the platter down on a stool near the fire. It contained hot meat and bread, and at the sight of it Richard swallowed convulsively. In spite of his grief he was hungry, for the Baron and his party had only stopped once for refreshment during the ride, and then Richard had been unable to do more than make a pretense of eating. But now, calmed by the warmth and comfort of Sir Hugo's room and cheered by the company of this little girl who smiled at him in a shy but friendly way, he drew the knife from its sheath on his belt and set to. Alys sat down sedately on the carpet and watched him while he ate. When he had finished, he looked ruefully at the grease on his hands and she said quickly:

"I should have brought water and a napkin, but I couldn't carry any more. If you will wait a minute, I will fetch them."

"You should not wait on me," protested Richard. "Who are you? You are not a serving wench?"

"The Earl of Banworth is my uncle," said the little girl. "My mother was his sister, but she—she is dead, and my father went to the Crusades and never returned. My uncle gives me a home and is very kind."

"And your aunt?" inquired Richard curiously. "Is she kind too?"

The little girl's face grew pink. She hesitated, and then, ignoring his question, said: "I will fetch the water. Do not wipe your hands on your hose while I am gone." She disappeared, and Richard grinned.

How had she known what he was about to do? He looked at his greasy fingers and sucked them thoughtfully. They tasted pleasantly of roast pork.

In a very few moments Alys returned. She kicked the door gently and called: "Open, please. My hands are full."

Richard opened the door and took the bowl of water from her. He washed his hands and face and dried them on the towel she held out to him. The linen was the finest he had ever seen and the bowl was of brass, and not crock, like the washing bowls at home. It was all very grand.

"Have you had your supper, Alys?" he inquired, setting down the bowl and folding the towel neatly as his mother had taught him to do.

Alys made a face. "I have eaten," she said, "but not down there in the hall. I hate sitting at the high table with everyone staring at me. And I hate all that food, and the way my uncle and the other men eat. They gnaw their meat like dogs and their beards shine with grease. So I'll tell you what I do. I creep out to the buttery and I get what I like best from old Nicholas, who is the House Steward, and I take it away somewhere quiet and eat alone."

"What does your aunt say to that?" said Richard. "Is she not cross?"

Alys hung her head, and her long, fair hair hid her face.

"She does not care what I do," she said in a low voice. "She tells me to keep out of her sight. I think she—hates me."

"Why?" asked Richard bluntly.

"Because she hated my mother, who was m'lord's favorite sister, and so my aunt was jealous. She *is* jealous, you know. She would have everyone to love her best. But you cannot love her, or at least I cannot."

"Do you love Louis?" asked Richard. "He is your cousin, and that is next best thing to a brother."

"You ask too many questions," said Alys quietly, and her small face looked suddenly old and sad. "Tell me about you, instead. I know only that my uncle brought you here as a prisoner, or hostage. He says you are to be a page, and my aunt is very angry. Have you a father and mother, and sisters and brothers at home?"

Richard turned away from her so that she should not see his face. He hunched up his shoulders and clasped his hands around his knees.

"My father disappeared during the fighting," he said huskily. "I know not if he is alive or dead. No one seems to know. It is a mystery. My mother lies abed with my little sister, who is only a few days old. I have no other near kin."

"How dreadful for you," said Alys soberly. "It must be so wonderful to have a little baby sister and—and a mother. I was only three years old when my mother died, and I do not remember her at all. But your father—how could he disappear? Someone must know what became of him?"

"They do not," said Richard positively. "At least, I mean, the enemy do not know. Old Odo—that's a minstrel who visits us and who was in the Hall when your uncle broke through our defenses—he overheard your uncle and his knights talking, and they do not know where my father went after he fell from his horse. Odo says that maybe a miracle occurred, but that I cannot believe."

"But if he were dead, it would be known," argued Alys.

She put out a hand and laid it comfortingly on Richard's arm. "He must be alive and someone has hidden him. I think you have good reason for hope, Richard."

"If he is alive, he will come and rescue me from this hateful place!" cried Richard.

Alys hung her head even lower and a tear dropped on the bright blue of her gown.

"No one will ever rescue me," she said in a low voice. "I shall live here until I am old enough to marry and then I am to wed the Count of Clairembault, because my uncle desires the family connection. The Count is old. I am to be wed when I am twelve, which is three years from now, and by then he will be more than forty! I shall have to go away and live in a foreign land. Oh, Richard, the thought of it frightens me so much!"

Richard could not think what to say. However hard his own lot, at least no one could make him marry against his will and carry him off to live among foreigners in a strange land. In one way at least he was better off than this poor little girl. He liked Alys. He had never known a girl before— at least not a girl of his own rank with whom he could be friends. To have her as a companion in misfortune would be a comforting thing indeed. Timidly, he reached out and clasped her hand and they sat together in silence, while the burning logs purred on the hearth and then broke sharply, sending out blue flames, for the wood was driftwood, recovered from the sea.

The sound of the door opening startled them both and they jumped up nervously, but it was only Sir Hugo, who smiled at them and said: "Well, my little friends, and so you have become acquainted. Did Richard eat his supper, Alys?"

"Yes, sir, he did," said Alys, smiling up into the tall man's face. "He ate every bit, and I brought him water afterward to wash his hands."

"That was well done," said Hugo. He sat down in his big chair and stretched wearily. "It has been a long day," he said. "Richard, you must be ready to sleep."

"I am not sleepy at all," said Richard stoutly. "Please, Sir Hugo, tell me what they say of me down there in the hall. Lady Eleanor said I was to be sent to the kitchens, but Alys says I am to be a page."

"There is no question of your being sent to the kitchens or put to any other menial work," said Sir Hugo. "Lady Eleanor spoke in the heat of her temper. She knows very well that m'lord will respect your rank. You are to be a page in the household, and treated in every respect as are the other pages, except insomuch as you are younger than the other two and so your duties will be less onerous. No doubt, Richard, your father intended sending you away to some other noble house when you were a little older? It is the custom, as you well know."

"The other two pages come from noble families," put in Alys. "Henry is nearly fourteen and leaves here soon to return home to Northumberland, and John is a nephew of the Earl of Leicester himself. My uncle considers it a great honor to have been entrusted with a kinsman of the great de Monfort."

"They are all traitors and enemies of the King," said Richard morosely. Alys grew red.

"If you are going to talk like that, how can we be friends?" she said.

"Alys is right," said Sir Hugo gently. "Leave politics and

wars to your elders. Children can set an example to them by showing only brotherly love. Hatred should not lodge in young hearts."

"I am sure hatred lodges in Louis's heart," retorted Richard. "There is little brotherly love to be expected from that quarter."

"Louis is a spoiled and unhappy boy," said Sir Hugo sadly. "His father is too often from home and the boy is dominated by his mother. M'lord of Banworth is much taken with your manliness, Richard, and desires that you shall be his son's companion. Try to fall in with his wishes, for your own sake. Sometimes it is more expedient to go with the tide. Soon these wretched, unsettled times will be over and you will see your mother and your home once more. In the meantime, try to be content, and reflect that it is not every boy who has the chance to live in one of the most splendid castles in the land."

"Content?" cried Richard. "Content, when I know nothing of my father's fate? Oh, Sir Hugo, please, tell me what you think has happened to my father. If you have certain knowledge of his death, tell me. I would rather know the truth."

"My poor boy, if I knew I would tell you," said Sir Hugo earnestly. "No one here knows, and that is the truth. There is some mystery that is yet to be solved. He is not dead, to our knowledge, and he has not been taken prisoner. When he fell from his horse, his own men closed in around him and fought like tigers. When they were—dispatched—your father had vanished. That is all we know."

There was silence in the small room. The fire crackled and purred, a sudden flurry of rain beat against the closed shutters, and a mouse, encouraged by the quiet, ventured out from behind a chest, seized upon a crumb dropped from

Richard's supper, and scurried back to its hole. Alys looked sympathetically at Richard, and Richard stared into the heart of the fire. Suddenly, the long, anxious, tiring day took its toll of him, his head dropped on to his chest, and he fell profoundly asleep.

When he awoke, Alys had gone and he was lying on a soft, feather-filled palliasse, covered by a fur-lined rug. He felt so warm and comfortable that he only half opened his eyes, saw dimly Sir Hugo's tall figure standing near him, and fell once more deeply into sleep.

He came to his senses slowly with the morning light and lay for a time wondering where he was. The window seemed to be in the wrong place, and a shaft of bright sunlight shining like a sword-blade between the shutters struck on the rich colors of the carpet and the wide hearth, where the fire had burned itself into a heap of gray ash. Turning his head, he saw Sir Hugo, still sleeping in the bed nearby, his gray head cushioned on a scarlet, tasseled pillow. His face, in the morning light, looked tired and old. From outside came the sound of horses' feet and a great baying of hounds. Richard remembered the two wolfhounds, Shamus and Tara, and in spite of his anxiety and sorrow he felt a lifting of the heart. They were such splendid dogs, and he looked forward to meeting them again.

Slipping cautiously off the chest, he tiptoed over to the window and carefully, inch by inch, unfastened the bar which secured the shutters. He opened one shutter a few inches and peered out. Then he gasped in astonishment, and forgetting all caution, flung the shutters wide and leaned out of the narrow window as far as he dared go.

It was a perfect morning, warm as spring. The earth steamed in the warmth of the sun, smelling deliciously.

Somewhere near at hand, Richard guessed, there must be an herb garden, for the air was spiced with the scent of rosemary and thyme. From the stables, men and lads were leading out horses to water them at the stone troughs which stood near a pump in the center of the inner ward. Two couples of greyhounds played on the grassy slope which led down to the barbican, while Shamus and Tara, aloof and splendid, watched their gambols with calm disdain.

Servants were everywhere, hurrying on errands to cookhouse and store. Soldiers sat in the sun cleaning armor, boys staggered past almost hidden under bundles of hay and straw as big as themselves. The handle of the pump kept up a steady clank-clank, and a man whistled a lilting tune, his whistle as high and clear as a bird's.

But it was not the men or the animals which held Richard's eye and made him cry out so that Sir Hugo stirred and woke. It was the sea, the huge, shining, bright blue sea, stretching away, calm and still, to the farthest limits of the world! And there too was the splendid ship—was it the same or another?—her white sails spread, skimming before the light wind like the seagulls that swooped and cried above the castle walls.

"Oh!" Richard cried. "Oh!"

Turning from the window, he seized his clothes and pulled them on at top speed, his fingers fumbling impatiently with the strings which held up his breeches. He fastened the belt around his tunic, drew on his shoes, and made for the door, intent only on gaining the outside world and finding his way down to the very brink of the wonderful sea. He glanced at the bed in passing, but Sir Hugo had his eyes shut and was pretending to be asleep. Richard, Sir Hugo reflected, had to leave the sanctuary of his room some time and face his new world, and as well now as later.

The door which led to the outside stair stood open, and Richard ran down the steps to the bailey. A few people looked at him curiously, but no one spoke or tried to stop him until he reached the gateway between the inner and outer wards. This also stood open, but as he tried to pass through, a hand grasped him by the arm and a rough voice said: "Not so fast!"

"Let me go!" cried Richard, wriggling.

"What—and have you run away and give us all a deal of trouble to find you and bring you back?" demanded the man. "I know you, my lad. You're the young whelp we brought with us yesterday. A prisoner, that's what you are, and don't you forget it."

Richard stared at the man in astonishment. He was an ordinary soldier, that much was evident from his clothes, and no common man had ever dared to speak to him in such a tone before! All his pleasure in the bright day died, as the complete change in his circumstances was brought home to him in full force. Miserably, he shook himself free of the man's grip and, turning, set out back across the bailey toward the towering walls of the keep.

A shout halted him, and he waited as two boys, older than himself, came running toward him. One of them had fiery red hair and a round, good-tempered face, the other was thin and dark with heavy, black eyebrows which looked strange on so young a face. Both boys were dressed alike in dark green surcoats with fur at the neck and sleeves. Richard guessed them to be the two pages, Henry and John. They stopped short when they came up with him, staring at him curiously.

"Are you the prisoner, Richard Travers?" demanded the boy with the heavy brows. Richard nodded, waiting warily for what would come next.

"Your father was for the King, was he not?" put in the round-faced boy. "We are told that he is now dead, and his castle is in our hands."

"So perish all traitors!" taunted the dark boy. "Long live Simon de Montfort, and God defend the right!"

Richard's temper rose, hot and fiery. He hit out, and caught the dark boy on the nose. The boy gasped, then hit back, and Richard felt an agonizing stab of pain in his right eye. He struck out again, the red-headed boy thrust out a foot and tripped him up, and the next moment they were sprawling on the ground in a complicated, threefold heap.

6

A Surcoat Trimmed with Vair

"Now then, now then!" came a man's voice from above their heads. "Stop it at once, you young cubs!"

The two strange boys let go of Richard and got sheepishly to their feet. Their smart clothing was covered in mud, the taller boy's nose was bleeding freely, and the redhead had a rapidly swelling bump on his forehead where it had come in contact with Richard's foot. Richard himself remained on the ground, dazed and sick from the pain of his blackened eye. A strong hand caught him by the arm and jerked him to his feet. Looking up, he saw the stern face of the Captain of the Guard.

"Fighting!" said the Captain, looking from one dilapidated figure to the next. "You pages do nothing but fight! What will my lady say when she sees the state of your gear? In ten minutes' time you are due in the Great Hall, clean and neat, to wait upon m'lord and the rest of the company when they break their fast."

"By Our Lady!" exclaimed the older boy, and set off for the keep at a run, the younger boy following closely behind. Richard stayed where he was, uncertain whether he too would be required to carry out his new duties as a page in the Great Hall.

"What shall I do?" he inquired tentatively. The Captain looked down at the small, muddy figure and smiled.

"I advise you also to wash," he said. "And ask one of the women to find you unguents for your black eye. It will not endear you to Lady Eleanor if she thinks you are a fighter. You might attack her ewe lamb, and that would be a capital offense!"

"Do you mean Louis?" asked Richard. "The Baron has said I am to study with Louis, and learn manly sports."

The Captain laughed loudly.

"Manly sports!" he exclaimed. "Louis! His mother had rather he learned to ply the needle like a girl, save for the danger that he might prick his finger and swoon at the sight of blood. But there—he is m'lord's son and I should not speak so. Perhaps you and he will agree well enough. Take a tip from me," he added more kindly. "Make it your business to agree. Your position here is not enviable, for your happiness depends upon the whim of Lady Eleanor and the good will of her son."

"The Baron will see I am not ill-used," protested Richard. "And Sir Hugo is my friend."

"The Baron and Sir Hugo may ride out again soon," the Captain told him. "It cannot have escaped your notice that these are troublous times."

Richard blushed at the sarcasm in the man's voice.

"It would be difficult for me to forget it," he said in a low voice, "seeing that I myself am a prisoner of war."

"Ah, well, it's a hard life," said the Captain carelessly, and walked away. Richard hesitated a moment, then slowly made his way toward the outside stair which led to the upper floor and Sir Hugo's room. His eye ached abominably and he longed to follow the Captain's advice and find a woman to tend him. At home his nurse had used a poultice of lily leaves for bruises. She pounded them in a mortar and applied the resulting paste, laid on cool linen, to the hurt. He thought wistfully of her familiar touch and the sound of her voice. All his exhilaration and excitement caused by the new surroundings quite vanished, and as he climbed the stairs he had once again to struggle with his tears.

"So there you are!" said a sharp voice as he reentered the upper floor of the keep, and he looked up to see an elderly woman regarding him severely. She was dressed very simply and was obviously no grand lady, though her linen wimple was as snowy as Lady Eleanor's own.

"Where have you been?" she demanded, and went on without waiting for a reply. "I have been watching for you a full half hour. My lady has given orders that you are to be fitted with a green surcoat like the other pages. I have one which has been outgrown by Henry, and will do very well for you. Oh, you need not turn up your nose! It is made of linsey-woolsey and the trimmings are of vair. I'll be bound you've never worn any fur other than rabbit or sheepskin. Vair is too good for boys, even pages in such a household as this, but there—everything here is twice as rich as anywhere else in the land." She stopped talking and peered more closely at Richard's face. "Why, what have you done to your eye? It is black and blue. Have you been fighting, you wicked little boy?"

"The dark boy taunted me and I hit him, and he hit me back," said Richard sullenly. "It was not my fault."

"Fault or not, you are in no state to wait on m'lady!" cried the woman. She seized Richard's arm and shook him hard. "You are a troublemaker, like all your kind. You should be locked in a cell, not allowed to mix with decent folk!"

The door behind them opened and Sir Hugo came out. He looked in silence at Richard's scowling face and his rapidly blackening eye before he said: "More trouble, Richard? I have warned you of the consequences of your unguarded temper. Go now with Dame Cicily and do as she bids you."

"It is not fair!" cried Richard, wriggling free from Dame Cicily's clutch. "Those boys called me a traitor! If they call me foul names I shall fight them! Sir Hugo, you cannot expect me—

"I expect you to control yourself," said Sir Hugo sternly. "You do not sufficiently realize your position here. The Baron is treating you far more generously than he has need to do, and you reward him by insulting his lady wife and brawling with his pages. It will not do, Richard. You must submit."

"I should think so indeed," chimed in Dame Cicily. "It seems the followers of King Henry have an ill way of raising their families! I have heard that little Prince Henry and his sister are two of the most spoiled children in the land, and their establishment at Windsor quite absurd in its grandeur. Overindulgence of children leads to hot blood and ill temper, until we get little monsters like this!"

Richard looked from Sir Hugo to Dame Cicily and back to Sir Hugo, whom he had thought to be his friend. In both faces he saw nothing but disapproval. Listlessly he turned away, saying, "I understand. I am to be called a page but in truth I am a prisoner, to be treated as such. I had as soon wear gyves as a surcoat trimmed with vair."

"Now you are talking foolishly," said Sir Hugo, smiling for the first time. "I have told you before, Richard, war is not for children. You are no prisoner, and you can yet be happy if you will allow yourself to be. Dame Cicily, be gentle with the lad," he added in a lower tone. "He is homesick and fatherless. Show him Christian charity."

"Come then," said Dame Cicily in gentler tones, and she led the way to a room full of rich clothing hanging from pegs on the walls. Selecting a small green surcoat, she handed it to Richard, together with clean hose and an undertunic of creamy-white linen. She bathed his bruised eye with a lotion which took much of the pain out of it, and combed his tousled hair into neatness.

"There!" she said at last. "Now you are fit to be seen. I am sorry if I was short with you, but my lady has done nothing but grumble and complain at me since I rose this morning, and in truth my own temper wears thin at times. You are only a little lad and not to blame for the sins of your elders. Now, be a good boy, do not fight, obey your betters, and hold your unruly tongue, then you will do well enough. Come to me if you are sick, or if you need clean gear. I am Louis's nurse, but I give an eye to the pages as well, since Louis is now a great lad and needs me less than he used to do."

"What shall I do now?" asked Richard. "I don't know where to go, or what duties are expected of me."

"Go down to the Great Hall and find Henry and John," said Dame Cicily. "Make your peace with them and they will instruct you in your duties. I believe this morning they are to have a lesson in swordsmanship together with Louis, if he feels in the mood for instruction. Come, that will not be so bad, will it? Every true boy loves to play with weapons just as every little girl loves her dolls."

"I wish I could see Alys," said Richard wistfully, and Dame Cicily said, "In due course. She creeps around the keep like a little mouse, that one. Poor child, her position here is little better than your own, although she has great riches in trust for her and when she marries she will be the chatelaine of a castle almost as fine as this, if what I hear be true."

"She doesn't want to be married," said Richard. Dame Cicily clicked her tongue disapprovingly.

"Doesn't want this—doesn't want that!" she exclaimed. "Children must do as they are bid. Run along now, before my patience is quite gone!"

Richard went out of the room and hesitated. It was going to be an ordeal to enter the Great Hall and meet the unfriendly eyes of Lady Eleanor, of Louis, and of the two pages. He wished he had not quarreled with them, but it was too late now for regrets. Very slowly he walked down the passage, past Sir Hugo's door, and descended the outside staircase once more. He paused again in the sunshine, watching a soldier polish his pike. The man looked up and gave him a friendly wink, then bent again to his task.

The doors which led to the Great Hall stood open, but the hall itself was shielded by an inner screen which reached almost from wall to wall and formed a kind of vestibule while at the same time protecting the hall from the draft. From behind the screen Richard heard the sound of many voices and the clatter of dishes. The household was breaking its fast, and Richard realized with a stab of hunger that he himself had eaten nothing since the night before. Timidly he walked around the screen and entered the hall.

On a dais at the far end of the enormous room sat the Baron and his Countess and the members of their household who ate with them. Louis was there too, and Sir Hugo, while Henry and John, looking as if butter would not melt in their mouths, stood behind the Baron's chair. John held a silver

basin of water and Henry a linen towel. In the main part of
the hall the long trestle tables and benches had already been
cleared away, for the lesser members of the household had
eaten earlier and had now gone about their work. The two
wolfhounds drowsed in front of the hearth fire, stretched out
on the rushes of the floor. A sweet smell came from the
strewing herbs, reminding Richard sharply of his own home.
Then one of the dogs sensed a newcomer and sat up, his tail

going thump-thump on the floor as he recognized Richard as a friend. The sound caught the attention of the company at table and there was a sudden hush while every eye turned on the small, lonely figure by the door. For a moment shyness and dread almost overcame Richard and he would have given much to turn and run. Then a voice inside his head seemed to murmur "Courage—high courage!" and he walked quietly up to the dais and bowed, first to the Baron and then to Lady Eleanor, his wife.

The Baron leaned across the table, the leg of a fowl clutched in his hand, and peered at Richard's face. Then he chuckled delightedly.

"So! What have we here—a young fighting cock!" he exclaimed.

"Disgraceful!" said Lady Eleanor. "The boy is a barbarian. I told you what it would be, m'lord, if you allowed such a child into our home. If he should turn his spite on Louis—"

"Of course he will do no such thing," said the Baron hastily.

"He had better not!" whined Louis. "Father, tell him he is not to touch me. Mother—tell m'lord that I do not want this boy near me!"

Everyone began to talk at once, with Louis's voice, shrill and hysterical, rising above the rest. Richard stood quite still, hating everyone and despising Louis with all his might. Louis was older than he, and taller, and yet he was afraid! He looked at the two pages, who stood behind the Baron's chair, and was amazed to see them fighting back their giggles. Their faces were red with effort and John's hands shook so that the water slopped out of the silver bowl and trickled down the back of the Baron's chair. They caught Richard's eye and grinned in a friendly way. Henry jerked his head toward Louis and made a face. Lady Eleanor turned around so sharply that she nearly caught them at it, and in a moment they were grave again, intent upon their work.

But Richard felt altogether different. Perhaps, after all, every man's hand was not against him. Perhaps the boys would be friendly and he would have allies against the unpleasantness of Lady Eleanor and her son. Then the Steward came forward and directed him fussily to take his place behind the table with the other pages, and he gave him a pile of clean linen napkins to hold bidding him hand one to such of the company as required it. He stood between John and Henry, exchanging shy smiles with them, and performed his duties with them until the meal was over. No one took any more notice of him, and to his great relief the Baron, Lady Eleanor, and Louis left the hall without anything further being said. When everyone had gone, the boys fell to on what remained of the meal, washing it down with weak ale. The food was good, and Richard ate hungrily. He wondered where Alys was and if she had eaten her breakfast in some quiet corner, like the little mouse Dame Cicily had called her. He longed to see Alys again.

"Now then, you boys, be off with you and let the table be cleared," exclaimed the Steward impatiently. Richard washed his hands in the water left in the silver bowl and dried them on the last of his clean napkins. Then he followed Henry and John out into the brightness of the inner ward.

"We've decided to be friends with you," said John gravely. "Henry and I talked it over and we've decided not to hold it against you that your father was a—" He stopped abruptly as Henry gave him a warning look, and ended lamely, "that your father was on the other side."

"We respect your courage," chimed in Henry, tenderly

feeling his nose. "You are only a little fellow, yet you took us both on at once and gave quite a good account of yourself. That commands respect."

"Thank you," said Richard. "I—er—you do understand I cannot allow anyone to speak ill of my father? If we are to be comrades, that must be understood."

"It is understood," said John. Unseen by Richard, he winked at Henry, and went on solemnly, "All insults to be wiped out in blood."

"If necessary," added Henry cautiously.

"But only among ourselves," added John. "From Louis I very much fear you will have to accept insulting behavior with Christian resignation. Blood does not agree with Louis, it makes him sick, and if Louis is sick my Lady Eleanor is like a lioness with an injured cub. Now, one may fight men, but what defense has a gentleman against the wrath of the fairer sex?"

"Does he always talk like that?" asked Richard, turning to Henry, half amused and half bewildered. Henry laughed.

"Our red-headed friend fancies himself at rhetoric," he said. "Try to cut through the flowers of his speech and find the sense, because he gives you good advice."

"Everyone keeps telling me the same thing!" exclaimed Richard. "But it seems to me that try as I will I shall never please Louis or his mother. They are determined to hate me."

The other two boys were silent. It seemed they could find nothing comforting to say. After a pause, Richard asked: "Where is Alys?"

"Who knows?" said John carelessly. "Or wait, perhaps Henry knows. He is ever attentive to the little mouse be-cause he has hopes that when she is married to the Count de

Clairembault she will use her influence with her husband to obtain for Henry a place at the French King's court. He is a farsighted lad, our Henry."

"You talk nonsense," said Henry shortly, but his face grew red. "How come you to know Alys, Richard?"

"She brought supper to me in Sir Hugo's room last night," Richard told him. "We talked, and I liked her."

"She is a sweet little maid," said Henry. "I am sorry for her, for she is another whom Lady Eleanor hates."

"Still, she is to make a splendid marriage," said John. He rubbed a hand over his red hair until it stood up on end, and went on enviously, "Her future husband is one of the richest men in France, richer even than my uncle, the Earl of Leicester."

A shadow fell between the boys and the sun and they looked up to see the burly figure of their fencing master standing before them.

"You pages gossip like women!" he exclaimed disapprovingly. "Come with me, and I will find you a more manly way of passing the time." He turned to Richard and went on kindly, "Have you had instruction in swordsmanship? You have? Good! It seems that you are not such a little barbarian as some people would have us believe."

"He is a fine fellow," said John. "Take no heed of his politics, sir, for his heart is in the right place and we have sworn friendship, aye, and sealed the bond of brotherhood in blood!"

"Chiefly Henry's blood!" put in Richard, remembering his lucky blow on the dark boy's nose. He began to giggle helplessly at his own wit, the other two boys joined in, and they rolled about the courtyard, weak with laughter, while the fencing master stood looking at them with a sardonic but patient smile.

7

A Plan Is Born

Winter gave place to spring, with green shoots and bird song. Summer came, and the sea sparkled under a hot sun. Richard had been nearly five months at the castle now. He had grown taller and graver and had learned many things, among them the hard task of keeping his temper when provoked.

Now it was high summer, and all over England there was an uneasy peace. The King and de Montfort were outwardly friends, for de Montfort's Parliament, which had sat from January until March, had achieved a formal truce. But Prince Edward remained a prisoner, and the King, people muttered, was little better than a prisoner himself. To thoughtful people the peace was a hollow sham, and they waited apprehensively for what might come next.

Meanwhile the red Baron and his knights remained at home and gave themselves up to the delights of the long summer days. Even Lady Eleanor looked less sour now the dark winter days were over. She had had the keep cleaned from end to end. Smoke-laden cobwebs were banished from high ceilings, and men with paint and limewash invaded the Great Hall, so that for a week the household ate in the solar, or in their own apartments if they chose.

Sir Hugo was one of those who chose to eat alone, for he was not well. He had had a fever in the last harsh cold of March, and recovered slowly, complaining of pain in his limbs. Richard waited on him, bringing him such food as he could eat, and possets and herbal drafts from the stillroom. Alys, too, came in and out and kept him company, so that Richard saw more of her than he had managed to do before.

"I like her best of all the people here," he told Sir Hugo in a burst of confidence one day. "After you, sir, that is. I like Henry and John very much, but they are older than I am and they never let me forget it. Besides, they are such friends they do not really want a third. But Alys has no one but me. She is like a sister to me."

"She is a dear little maid," agreed Sir Hugo.

"Louis pulled her hair today!" Richard told him angrily. "I was standing by and heard her cry out. I almost hit him. I wish I had."

"That would have done no good to either you or Alys," Sir Hugo said quietly. "I am glad you are learning to control your hot temper, my son."

"Shall I tell you how I have trained myself to forbear?" asked Richard. Sir Hugo nodded, smiling into Richard's eager face.

"I tell myself that Louis is sickly. To strike him would be like striking a woman. I say to myself, 'Leave him alone. He is a weakling and will never live to grow into a man.' "

"You may well be right," said Sir Hugo sadly. "Then the Baron will have no son, and no one knows better than I the sorrow that brings to a man. Your father was fortunate, Richard, for I think he may well have felt a little pride in you."

"Sir Hugo—" Richard hesitated, then went on, "I still believe my father to be alive."

"Greater marvels have been known," said Sir Hugo. "Certainly there is no proof of his death."

"Alys believes it too," said Richard. "She prays daily that one day I shall be reunited with my family."

"It is a good prayer," said Sir Hugo. "But remember, Richard, the Lord's ways are mysterious to us. Hope, but do not build too much on your hope. Strive to live as your father would have had you live, so that through you, if he is dead, he may live again in his son."

"He is alive!" said Richard stubbornly. "I know it."

Sir Hugo moved his head wearily on the cushion. He was sitting in his high-backed chair close before the fire, for even the bright sunlight did little to warm the stone-walled room.

"Go down into the courtyard and seek Crispin, the wagoner," he said. "He has been lately to Dorchester to fetch provisions and I have a great longing for some figs which I ordered him to purchase especially for me. He was due back today and I do not wish my packages to be taken to the spiceroom with the rest of the goods. If he has not yet arrived, wait below until he does. It will do you good to be out in this lovely summer air."

"If only I was permitted to ride Starlight, I could go to meet him," said Richard resentfully. "Starlight is my own palfrey and I am denied the use of him. It is by Lady Eleanor's orders. The Baron would not stoop to such small meanness. You say I am not a prisoner, but never, since I arrived, have I been permitted to cross the drawbridge, not even to go down on to the beach."

"In time, more freedom will be allowed you," Sir Hugo answered him. "You must be patient. You have been here less than five months."

"It seems like years," sighed Richard. "Well, I will wait for Crispin in the outer ward and then I can intercept him before he starts to unload." He hesitated a moment and then went on: "Do you think, Sir Hugo, it is possible Crispin may have heard news of my father? He must meet people from many parts of the country when he goes to Dorchester, and after all, my home is not so very far away."

"Try not to build your hopes, Richard," said Sir Hugo quietly. "Try to resign yourself to accepting your father's death, for dead I am convinced he is."

"Then why was his body not found!" cried Richard. "I will not accept his death, not until I am sure, and one day I will discover the truth."

"Do not slam the door!" said Sir Hugo quickly, but too late. The heavy oak door was pulled to with a shattering crash, and the sound of Richard's running feet died away down the long passage.

Crispin had just crossed the drawbridge when Richard arrived, breathless, in the barbican. The six great horses stood steaming in the mild air and soon the grooms were busy unharnessing them and leading them away to their well-earned rest. The wagon, loaded high with barrels and packages, bore traces of the muddy roads along which it had lately traveled. Crispin himself was seated on a grassy bank, his russet tunic grimed to his knees and his hose spattered with mud. In his hands he held a large wooden cup of ale from which he drank thirstily, for the day was warm and the last part of the way to the castle was all uphill. He looked up as Richard approached, and gave him a slow, warm smile. They were friends, these two, for once, in his youth, Crispin had lived near Richard's home and had known something of his family, so there was a bond between them, very precious to Richard in his homesick and lonely state.

"Well, young master," said Crispin in his slow, country-

man's drawl. "Have 'e come to hear all the gossip from Dorchester? There's been a fine wedding there, and a hanging. Aye, three villains was hanged for robbery on the king's highway and a good thing too, say I."

"Had you any adventures upon the road?" asked Richard eagerly. The old man shook his head.

"Naught worse than a cast shoe," he said. "But then I had two stout young fellows, well armed, to ride beside the wagon and keep us from harm. M'lord takes no risks when it comes to providing for his table, and this wagon contains some rare good ale, besides almonds and spices—cloves and cinnamon and ginger. Then there's m'lady's new cloak from the tailor's. Made of the finest camlet it is, and trimmed with miniver. A rich prize for a highway robber, that would have been, and I should not have cared to return home without it." He chuckled. "My neck is too precious to me. I value my neck, young master Richard. I love it well."

Richard laughed politely at the old man's rather gruesome joke. Then he said: "I am sent by Sir Hugo to fetch a special package you have for him."

"Aye, so I have, so I have," said Crispin. He drank the rest of the ale, turning the cup upside down over his face to catch the last drop, then he got slowly to his feet and began to unfasten the lashings which held down the heavy canvas wagon sheet.

"'Tis just in the corner here, I put it handy," he muttered. "Ah, here 'tis." He handed a bundle to Richard. "Tell Sir Hugo there was no figs to be had, so I brung 'im raisins and dates in place of 'em and I hope I done right."

"I'm sure you did," said Richard. "I'll tell him. Thank you, Crispin."

"Tell 'im if he wishes I'll try for his figs next time I go to

London," said the old man. "There's plenty of everything in London."

"You're going to London?" cried Richard in surprise. "Isn't it a very long way?"

"Aye, it is," said Crispin. "But every year I goes up to London to fetch m'lord's special wine which comes from his own vineyards in France. It always comes up London river and I fetch it from the wharf just below Blackfriars. Why the ship cannot put into Poole, which is but a few miles from here, I know not, but so it is. Them Frenchies have their own way of doing things. So, I goes up with the biggest wagon with just a boy or two to help me with the horses, and down I comes again, rich laden, with four or five pikemen to guard the wine."

"If you go to London," said Richard wistfully, "you must pass quite near to my home."

"That I do," said Crispin. "You can just see the towers of your home from rising ground not five miles away. Then the road dips down into the forest—"

"I know it well," sighed Richard. "It was in that forest my father used to hunt the deer." He turned away and said huskily, "I must take the package to Sir Hugo now, he will be waiting."

Crispin watched the small figure run across the bailey and climb the stair. He shook his head slowly and muttered, "Poor little lad, poor fatherless little lad!"

As Richard came out of Sir Hugo's room again, he stood indecisive, wondering what to do. The pages had been given a rare holiday and Henry and John had gone out with the falconer to fly the falcons at crows. Richard had wanted to go with them, but Lady Eleanor, for no good reason that Richard could see, had forbidden him to go. Now, before he had time to escape, she descended upon him and ordered him to join Louis in the garden of the keep. Louis, as usual, was sickly and unable to do much except play in a desultory way at ball. Richard pitied him and tried to be patient and kind, but it was difficult. Louis was so overbearing and said such hurtful things.

He found him now sitting on a stone bench under the nut trees, playing at cat's cradle with Alys. Alys's face was flushed and she looked as if she had been crying. Richard felt his temper rise. If Louis had been pinching her again, he would—he knew not what, in the heat of his temper, he might not do.

"So here you are at last," said Louis as Richard approached the bench. "Where have you been?"

"I had an errand to perform," said Richard shortly. "Sir Hugo sent me to see old Crispin, who is just returned from Dorchester."

"And you lingered, talking to a serving man!" taunted Louis. "No doubt you feel more comfortable in the presence of varlets?"

Richard reddened and Alys said quickly: "Louis, pray don't."

"Don't what?" asked Louis in feigned surprise. "Do you not wish me to show interest in the pleasures of my household, Alys? I am happy that Richard should have had converse with one of his own kind."

"You know Richard is nobly born," said Alys reproachfully. Louis laughed loudly.

"He is the son of a dead traitor—" he began and then paled as Richard shot out a hand and gripped him by the arm.

"Touch me and I tell my mother!" he whined. Richard let go so suddenly that Louis nearly fell back off the bench.

"Your lady mother says you wish to play at ball," said Richard between clenched teeth.

"I no longer wish to play," muttered Louis. He shot Richard a spiteful look and went on, "You have made me ill, shaking me so."

"Oh, Louis!" Alys cried. "He did not shake you, he only gripped your arm, and you were provoking, you know you were!"

"I feel ill," Louis repeated. "I have a pain *here*." He laid his hand to his side. "I am going to find my nurse." Getting up, he went slowly back to the keep, leaving an uncomfortable silence behind him.

"More trouble, I suppose," said Richard gloomily. "Lady Eleanor believes every word he says. Oh, Alys, I am so tired of being scolded! Every single thing I do is sure to be wrong!"

"It is the same with me," said Alys sadly. "It seems as if those two must have someone to hate."

"If it is like this now, what will it be like when the Baron is no longer here?" said Richard. "He at least is fair and m'lady dare not go too far for fear we may complain to him. But when he is gone—oh, Alys, what shall we do?"

There was a long silence. Overhead in the nut trees birds chirped gaily; bees from nearby hives worked busily among the flowers. The warm sun drew out the good scent of the herbs, and a light wind brought with it wheeling gulls and a smell of salt, fresh and invigorating. Far below where they sat, the sea sparkled and shone and the great stones of the wall were hot to the touch.

"Alys," said Richard at last. "Alys, have you ever thought of escape?"

Alys looked frightened. She glanced around quickly before replying.

"Escape? Why, Richard, what do you mean? How could you escape from here, and where would you go?"

"I would go home," Richard told her. "I would hide near my home and search for my father, for I do not believe him to be dead."

"You at least have a home," said Alys soberly. "I have no home but this. Where would I go if I—escaped?"

"Well, no, I suppose you could not escape," admitted Richard. Suddenly he brightened. "You could accompany me!" he exclaimed. "Oh, Alys, it is a splendid idea! You could dress as a boy and together we would hide in the forest near my home and seek news of my father. Crispin was speaking of the forest just now, and it came into my head how one might hide there for weeks and no one the wiser. It is summer now, with warm nights, so that one could sleep out of doors. I would build a little hut for you, Alys, and seek food—oh, say you will come! When I have found my father, he will think of some way of winning our castle back and then you can live there with us and never, never marry that old Frenchman. Would you not like that, Alys? You know you would!"

"Stop!" demanded Alys, half laughing and half crying. "You are talking wildly, Richard. You make it all sound like a game. How should we ever escape from here?"

"We could—" Richard thought desperately. He rose and, leaning over the wall which bounded the garden, gazed down into the bailey and then beyond, at the great expanse of sea. A ship was beating her way along the coast against the wind, bound for Poole harbor, and just offshore a small fishing boat swung at anchor. A boy leaned over the stern, a fishing line in his hand.

"If only we could make our way down to the shore and

conceal ourselves on a ship," Richard sighed. "That would be a fine way to escape."

"But we are never allowed to go down to the shore," said Alys sadly. "We are never allowed anywhere alone. I have only once been outside the walls since I was brought here, and that was when we all went to stay at my uncle's other castle near Deal, in Kent. It was such a long journey and the chariot in which I traveled with Louis and my aunt was so very uncomfortable. I had much rather have ridden my palfrey, but my aunt would not let me. The chariot rolled until Louis and I felt quite sick, and my aunt was cross all the time."

"I have just been talking to Crispin," said Richard dreamily. "He is often upon the road and he likes it. He told me that soon he goes to London to fetch wine, taking with him two boys to help with the horses—" He stopped abruptly and stared at Alys so strangely that she cried out: "What is it? What is the matter, Richard? Have you been stung by a bee?"

"Two boys!" repeated Richard, his eyes shining. "Do you not see, Alys? Here is our way of escape! We will bribe these boys to let us take their places. We will cut your hair and clothe you in rough, boy's gear, and no one will know it is you! I also will disguise myself in some way. I will wear a russet cloak and pull the hood well down over my face. Crispin always starts his journeys at dawn, so there will be few people about."

"But—will Crispin let us?" faltered Alys. "It is a splendid plan, Richard, but if Crispin should not agree—"

"Leave Crispin to me," said Richard confidently. "Have no fear, Alys, just leave all to me!"

8

A Voice in the Darkness

That night Richard could not sleep. He lay awake listening
to the sound of voices from the Great Hall below and
turning over and over in his mind his daring plan for escape.
When Sir Hugo at last came up to bed and the voices died
away, he was still awake, staring into the darkness, lying
very still so that Sir Hugo should not question him about his
wakefulness.

He knew what they had been talking about down below.
At the evening meal when he, with the other pages, had
been in attendance on the company, the talk had been all of
Prince Edward's daring escape from Earl Simon's custody in
Hereford. Richard could hardly wait until the meal was over
to find Alys and pour out the story to her.

"It was splendid, Alys!" he exclaimed, his eyes shining.
"What do you think he did? He got his friends to send in a
charger for his use, a wonderful beast, swift and strong.
Then he gained permission to ride out to exercise beyond the
city walls. Oh, he had a guard, of course, but he asked to try
their horses, one by one!"

"Why?" asked Alys, enthralled by the story but doubtful if
she should show joy at the escape of the Prince.

"To tire them, of course!" said Richard triumphantly. "He

galloped them hard and left them winded. Then, when all
were spent, he leaped upon the back of his new charger and
was away! The tired horses could not catch him and now he
is with the Earl of Gloucester at Ludlow, no doubt planning
to attack Earl Simon and recover his father the King, who is
the Earl's prisoner, although he does not call him so."

"I do not understand these things," said Alys. "I am glad
the poor Prince is no longer a prisoner, but it is horrible to
think there will be more fighting. I thought that it was all
over."

"Well, it is not," said Richard. "It is about to start again
more bitterly than before, and this time, please God, our side
will prevail. The Earl of Leicester must be in a great fright,
for he has sent word to your uncle to join him at Hereford as
soon as possible with all the men he can muster. Tomorrow
they prepare, and the day after they go."

Alys's eyes filled with tears. "Then we shall be left to the
mercy of my aunt," she said miserably. "Oh, Richard, if only
we could escape!"

Richard thought now of her small, unhappy face as he lay
sleepless on his bed. He knew she did not exaggerate the
gravity of their lot. With the Baron at home, Lady Eleanor
could do little except in minor ways to make the children's
lives a misery. The Baron was fond of Alys and amused by
Richard. He admired his pluck and made something of a pet
of him. Sir Hugo too was a powerful friend and his room a
refuge. But Sir Hugo was now well enough to accompany
the Baron into battle. In a very short time Richard would be
at the mercy of a merciless woman and her spiteful son.
Even his fellow pages would no longer be there, for John, to
his great excitement, was to accompany the Baron into
battle at the special request of his uncle, Simon de Montfort,

and Henry's time had come to return to his own home.
Already men had arrived to escort him to the North. Richard
would then be the only page in residence at Castle Banworth, his duty to wait upon Lady Eleanor. It was a
wretched prospect, and his resolve to escape became firmer
the more he thought of the matter.

In one way the absence of the Baron and his men would
make escape easier. John and Henry had told him how
different life was at the Castle when m'lord rode out to war.
Everything became slower and more easy. It was almost a
holiday for the people responsible for the daily running of
the household. The grooms and stable boys found their task
very different when the stables held, perhaps, fifty horses
instead of three hundred or more. The cooks and kitchen
lads—those who did not accompany the Baron—had only a
small household to feed, the Steward could rest a little from
his multitude of tasks. A quieter atmosphere prevailed, and
there would be time to enjoy the summer days. Time, that is,
for everyone but Richard. He guessed bitterly that his time
would be even more occupied than before. He would be at
the beck and call of Lady Eleanor and Louis from morning
till night.

All the more reason then to plan the escape!

Richard moved cautiously on his palliasse. His limbs were
cramped from lying still for so long. Sir Hugo stirred and
sighed but did not wake.

It was the two stable boys who must be approached and
persuaded to allow Richard and Alys to take their places at
the very last moment before the wagon rolled across the
drawbridge into the free world beyond. But how to persuade
them, that was the difficulty. Richard almost groaned aloud
as he realized he had nothing to offer as a bribe. And the

bribe would have to be a large one, for if it was discovered the boys had stayed behind willingly, their punishment would be severe.

Richard sat up and thumped his pillow into a more comfortable shape. A shaft of moonlight shone through the narrow window straight on to his face and he moved hastily aside, for it was well known that the moon's rays could send you mad.

Suppose the boys would not take the risk, no, not for any bribe? Such a contingency was more than likely, for the Baron had his moments of blind rage when all sense of right and justice was swallowed up in wrath and he would order a man or even a boy to be hanged, without a second thought. Lady Eleanor too would show small mercy to anyone who helped Alys to escape, even though she might consider herself well quit of her unwanted page. No, it would not be fair even to attempt to persuade the stable boys. They must be protected, somehow, from vengeance when the escape became known.

Trickery then? Tell the boys at the last moment that Crispin did not need them? It might work. Better still, persuade them into some outhouse which bore a stout lock and lock them in. That way suspicion would be averted from them, unless they were suspected of having received a bribe.

Richard's head spun. He was no further on. He still had no plan. He began to feel drowsy, but just as he was falling asleep a voice inside his head seemed to say clearly, "Put your trust in Crispin. It is your only hope." When he awoke hours later the words were still in his mind, and after he had performed his morning duties he went out to find Crispin and boldly lay the plan before him.

It was a chilly day with a light, mizzling rain blowing in

from the sea. Gulls mewed peevishly, lined up on the castle wall. Richard shivered and pulled his cloak more closely around him.

The inner bailey was humming with activity as the men got ready to ride out again to war. Soldiers were everywhere, and from the farriery came the clang of hammer on anvil and the acrid smell of scorching hooves. The great baggage wagons had been hauled out of their sheds for repairs. Many had iron strakes missing from their wheels and needed attention before they were again pressed into use. In an open-fronted shed Richard saw the knights' armor being burnished and chain mail repaired. Lady Eleanor herself was in the largest storeroom, superintending the packaging of special foods for the Baron and those nearest to him. Wine casks stood ready to be loaded, and salt meat in barrels. From the bakehouse came the mouth-watering smell of new bread, and the kitchen chimney poured out smoke as the cook and his scullions baked huge joints of fresh meat, to be eaten in the first few days. The grindstone whirred incessantly as swords, axes, and knives were sharpened to a razor's edge.

"Where are you all going?" Richard asked a soldier who, under cover of the chapel porch, was burnishing his lance with sand.

"It is no secret," the man replied. "Everyone knows that Prince Edward is at Ludlow. With the King himself still in Earl Simon's company it will be strange indeed if the Prince does not attack before long. We ride to join the Earl at Hereford, and somewhere in that region we shall meet Prince Edward's forces and do battle, if God wills it. Perhaps before the summer is over, the war too will be over and we can all return to our homes."

"Do you really think so?" asked Richard eagerly. The man smiled and shook his head.

"I am no prophet," he said. "I speak only out of the desire of my heart. All England is weary of war."

"I too," sighed Richard. "I too am weary of war." He left the soldier and went across to the stables, hoping to see Crispin, but when he at last ran him down in the wagon house the old man was busy and would not talk. He was greasing the axles of a baggage wagon and refused to allow Richard to help for fear he should stain his fine clothes.

"Be off now, Master Richard," he said crossly. "This is no place for pages. You must keep yourself nice, to wait on m'lady."

"But I want to talk to you," Richard protested.

"Then want must be your master," grunted the old man, and turned back to the pot of grease. Richard sighed and wandered off again. He was bursting with his plan of escape and longed to discuss it, but he had to admit that there is a time and a place for everything and the time was not yet, nor the place such a hub of activity as the wagon shed. He went in search of John and found him watching the armorers, one of whom was working on a small suit of chain mail for John's own use. The red-headed boy looked excited and slightly apprehensive. He glanced at Richard absently as though he hardly remembered who he was, and when Richard spoke he ignored him and turned instead to the armorer with eager questioning.

There was no companionship to be found there. Henry too was unapproachable, being closeted with Dame Cicily, going over his gear. Henry could hardly wait for the morning when he and his father's men would set out for the North, riding the first part of the way with the Baron's forces. Richard felt bitter envy for this boy who would so soon be back in the midst of his own family. It made him feel lonelier than before.

Sitting down on a stone, he buried his chin in his hands and gave himself up to thought. In all the months since he had left his home, no news had leaked through of his father's fate. Every time a traveling minstrel arrived at the castle, Richard looked at him eagerly in hopes that it might be Odo, with news of home. It never was. Perhaps by now the old man was dead.

The little sister, if she had lived, would be nearly half a year old. Had she fair curls, like her mother, and her father's blue eyes? Perhaps she looked like him, Richard, and reminded their mother of the son who was gone.

And the hounds—did they remember him still and wonder why he never came to the kennels to visit them any more? The house dogs would miss him sadly, for he had been the one to feed them and pet them and take them out. When he rode Starlight, it was always with three dogs at his heels, Rough the terrier, Trusty the old greyhound, and the spaniel, called in jest Mistress Stout. If Mistress Stout was not regularly exercised, her greed would be her undoing and she would die of a dropsy. Perhaps she too was dead.

Miserably, Richard rose and wandered into the Great Hall, which was full of knights assembling their gear. Here he was pounced upon by the House Steward, who told him that m'lady was in a fine temper, having been calling for the services of a page for the last hour. Richard sighed and went with lagging feet to the storeroom, where he met with a stormy reception and a sharp box on the ear. From then on, he had no time for homesickness, for Lady Eleanor kept him busy all the rest of the day running errands to various parts of the castle as she and her women sorted and packed the food and clothing needed by a nobleman about to depart on a campaign of uncertain duration.

Late that night the preparations were completed by the light of torches. Before dawn the next morning the great company would be on its way.

Richard, too weary even to sleep, stood with Alys by his side watching the scene. It was a night of wind, a boisterous wind from the sea which tossed the flame from the torches into long scarlet tongues and sent the smoke swirling into the sky. Grotesque shadows of men ran over the ground and mingled with the shadow of the great wagons, loaded high with all the accouterments of war. From the stables the horses, excited by the bustle, stamped and whinnied, moving restlessly in their beds of straw. Stable boys, tired out by the long day of toil, slept in the straw almost among the horses' feet. Three hundred and fifty horses waited for the dawn. Three hundred men waited stoically for what the future would bring, victory or defeat, sweet life or a cruel death; no man knew what lay ahead.

Someone laid a hand on Richard's arm and he started violently. His thoughts had been all of escape, and for a moment he imagined himself a fugitive and the grasp that of his captor. Then he saw that it was John, and laughed in his relief.

"Well, Richard," said the red-haired boy, and his usually cheerful voice was subdued. "This time tomorrow I shall be far from here, and so will Henry, and you will be left alone."

"He will have me," put in Alys timidly.

"And so he will, my little maid," said John kindly. "You two must hold together for mutual comfort. Richard, if I should not see you again, remember I always wished you well. Alys, when you are married, remember your old friend and invite me to visit you at your grand French château. That is—" he added with a sigh—"if I survive this campaign."

"Of course you will survive!" cried Richard, but John said, "That is as God wills. I am now accounted a man, and I take my chance with men."

There was a sudden silence. All at once John seemed removed from the other two by a barrier as high and strong as the castle walls. On one side lay childhood, on the other the dangerous, uncharted territory which was the grown-up world. Communication was no longer possible. Wordlessly they bade John farewell, and he wandered off into the darkness to join the men who would be his companions in the new life ahead.

Then Henry came, excited, bubbling over with joyful anticipation. His happiness was even harder for Richard to contemplate than John's apprehension, for Henry was going home. It was more than he could bear. He broke away from Henry and ran off into the darkness, intent only on being alone. Alys called after him but he took no notice, hurrying across the crowded bailey, dodging in and out of the men until he reached sanctuary in the now almost empty wagon shed. Here he leaned against the rough stone wall while dry sobs fought their way up into his throat and nearly choked him.

"Why, what's to do?" said a concerned voice. A light flickered and the voice went on: "If it isn't Master Richard! Whatever has happened to 'e, young sir? Are you hurt?"

"Oh, Crispin!" exclaimed Richard, recognizing the old man's voice. "Oh, I am so unhappy! I cannot bear my bondage any longer! I must, *must* escape and learn news of

my father. Crispin—please, *please* help me to escape!"

The old man gave a dismayed exclamation and dropped the light, which went out. Muttering, he felt about in the darkness until he held Richard by the arm. He drew him into the faint light which came through the open door, and peered earnestly into his face.

"Desperate, are ye?" he said quietly. "Aye, I can see in your face that you're ready to try desperate means. I'm not blaming ye, but as to helping ye, that's another kettle of fish. M'lord would stretch my neck if ever it was proved I helped his captive to escape. No, Master Richard, don't ask me. I'm an old man and I have a fancy to die quietly in my bed and not on the gallows, like a felon."

"He would never hang a faithful old servant like you!" exclaimed Richard. The old man nodded his head.

"He would hang me without a second thought," he said somberly. "Do you not know he hanged Peter, his oldest groom, because he let m'lord's favorite charger die of a quinsy? 'Twas not Peter's fault, but m'lord was so enraged he wanted someone to suffer, and Peter it was that died. Murder, I call it, but the law of the land admits his right. Given a cruel master, no man's life is safe."

"My father is not like that," said Richard. "Never would he hang his men."

"So I have heard," said old Crispin sadly. "Aye, so I have heard."

"Crispin," said Richard hesitantly. "If my father is alive, how would you like to serve him?"

"Well enough," said Crispin. "But I fear there is little hope your father is alive, and his castle is forfeit to the Earl of Leicester, so why waste breath on idle talk?"

A heap of straw in one corner of the shed rustled, and a hoarse voice spoke softly out of the blackness: "M'lord the Earl of Travers still lives!"

9

The Trumpets Sound for War

"By our Lady!" said Crispin in a startled voice. "Did you hear that, Master Richard?"

Richard, who had been doubting the evidence of his own ears, nodded dumbly, too surprised to speak.

The straw rustled again and a figure crept out and stood upright, the figure of an old man in rough clothes with long gray hair straggling over his shoulders. Even in the gloom of the wagon shed it was possible to see the white, sightless eyes.

"Odo!" exclaimed Richard. "Odo, is it really you?"

"Aye, it's me, young master," said the old blind minstrel. He turned back to the heap of straw and said to someone unseen, "Come out, and lead me to the door."

The straw stirred and parted as the small, wizened-faced boy wriggled out and took his blind master by the hand. He led him to where Richard stood, and stopped, yawning, half asleep on his feet.

"You—you said my father still lives?" questioned Richard eagerly. "Are you sure? How do you know?"

"It is a long story," said Odo, "and the boy and I are hungry, having traveled a long way since daybreak. We had thought to be made welcome here and given food, but

instead the Steward turned us away by m'lady's orders, saying that there was no time for such as I when the Baron is preparing to ride out to war. So instead of food and drink and a warm corner by the fire, we have nothing but a heap of straw, and no food has yet passed our lips."

"Wait, and I will bring food," said Crispin, and letting go Richard's arm, he hurried off to the kitchens, returning in a very few moments with bread and meat and a jug of ale. The small boy eyed the food wolfishly and retired to the straw with a great hunk of bread and the leg of a cold fowl. Richard himself attended to Odo's wants and guided the old man's hands to the food.

When he had eaten and drunk, and Richard was nearly at the end of his patience, Odo sighed with satisfaction, wiped his greasy hands with a wisp of straw, and said: "Now I feel better and can talk."

"Wait," said Crispin. He crossed to the door and looked cautiously all around. "It would not do if we were overheard. The Earl of Travers has no friends save ourselves within these castle walls."

Richard looked at him with sudden hope. If Crispin accounted himself a friend, then surely he must intend to help with the escape?

Eager questions rose to his lips, but before he could speak, Odo said: "I told you the Earl, your father, still lives, and this is true. I found him two weeks ago, living in a hovel deep in the forest not five miles from your home."

"In the forest?" cried Richard in amazement. "Why, what does he there? And how did he escape from death and his enemies? With my own eyes I saw him dragged from Pompey's back!"

"Aye, so he was," said the old minstrel. "So he was, and

almost done to death. His armor saved him, but it was also nearly his undoing, for, weighty as it is, he could not rise from the ground. Above him, men and horses surged to and fro while he lay as helpless as a turtle in its shell."

"Then how was he saved?" asked Richard impatiently.

"As others have been, by faithful friends," said Odo. "He was saved by men who loved him above their own lives. His knights and foot soldiers, seeing him helpless on the ground, closed in around him and fought desperately while one of their number, knowing of the secret passage, dragged him to the entrance, which was, fortunately, but a few yards away."

"Secret passage?" cried Richard. "I knew of no secret passage!"

"No doubt your father thought you too young to share the burden of secrecy," said Odo, and Crispin chimed in, "Very right too. The young should not be trusted with dangerous knowledge. Their tongues are too free."

"Never would I have divulged the secret," said Richard resentfully.

"He would have told you soon, no doubt," said Odo. "Perhaps on your twelfth birthday when no one could longer regard you as a babe."

"Well, perhaps," allowed Richard. "I am turned twelve now. My birthday passed unnoticed in this alien place. But where is this secret passage?"

"The entrance is in the chapel floor," said Odo. "I knew of it because when I was young and had my sight I helped in the construction. It was in your grandfather's time, aye, when your father was no more than a child. It is very close and narrow, allowing the passage of only one man at a time. Have you never noticed a stone in the chancel, marking the burial place of one John of Poitou, a monk?"

"Of course I have," said Richard. "What of him?"

Odo smiled.

"Never was there such a man, alive or dead," he said. "He was an invention of your grandfather's and his supposed burial spot is the entrance to the tunnel. The stone swivels on a pin and swings open, giving access to a small chamber beneath. From there the tunnel leads to a spot outside the castle walls. No one knew of this save I and your father and one trusted man, your father's body servant, who was at his side when he fell. Gregory is quick-witted and at once he bethought him of this sanctuary. He it was that rallied the men around m'lord, hastily bidding them to form a living screen behind which he could drag his master to the chapel door. God must have granted him more than human strength, for a man in full armor is no light weight to move."

He fell silent, and Richard said: "Could he not have helped my father to his feet?

"I have not told you all," said Odo quietly. "Never will your father stand on his own two feet again."

"Why not?" cried Richard in horror. "Odo—tell me quickly, why not?"

"Your father is crippled," said Odo. "A chance blow from a battle axe as he lay on the ground caught him across the knees and crushed the bones even through his armor. His suffering has been beyond measure terrible and he will never walk again."

"Oh, my poor father!" cried Richard in broken tones.

"How then did he escape?" queried Crispin.

"Gregory is the hero of the tale," Odo told him. "Once safely in the small chamber beneath the chapel floor, Gregory divested his master of his armor and tended the broken bones as best he could, binding both legs to m'lord's own broadsword, and padded with the quilted surcoat

which, as you know, is worn beneath chain mail. Thus
bound, the injured legs were at least less vulnerable, and he
could move his master, slowly and with care. Foot by foot he
eased him along the tunnel, and what were m'lord's suffer-
ings one shudders to think. Gregory himself was all but
spent when at last, under cover of night, they came forth
from the tunnel at the edge of thick woods. Then, after
resting, he carried m'lord upon his back to a hut deep in the
forest, a hut used by charcoal burners at certain times of the
year. There they have lived ever since."

"But why did not Gregory go for help?" cried Richard.
Odo shook his head.

"Your father cannot stand or walk," he said. "He relies on
Gregory for everything. How could he leave him? Besides,
the countryside is thick with enemies. Suppose Gregory
were captured? His crippled master would die lingeringly of
starvation. He judged it better to lie low, hunt for food, tend
his master, and wait for the Lord to send deliverance. He
little thought that the Lord's messenger would take the
shape of an old blind minstrel."

"You?" said Richard. "You will bring him deliverance? But
how?"

"Through you," said Odo quietly. "On you is the Hand of
the Lord."

"Me?" said Richard doubtfully. "Of course I will do anything to save my poor father, but what can I do?"

"I will tell you," said Odo. "You must make your escape
from here and go to the hut in the forest. I will tell you the
way. Once there, you can stay with your father while
Gregory goes to seek aid from others who fight for the King,
or, better still, you must go, for a nobleman will be more
swiftly roused to action, aye, and more trusting, if your

father's son himself is the messenger. A serving man might be an emissary of the enemy, a spy, but a child of noble blood would never be doubted. Yes, Master Richard, it will be for you to keep your courage high and undertake the hazardous quest."

Richard felt a small shiver of fear run down his back. Here at Castle Banworth he had been homesick and unhappy, but he had at least been safe. Now he was faced with a perilous journey of which he could not foresee the end. He felt suddenly small and young and the blood left his face, leaving him very white. But his voice when he spoke was steady.

"I am ready," he said. "Crispin, are you for me or against me in this enterprise?"

The old man rubbed a hand thoughtfully over his face. It made a rasping sound on his stubbly, unshaven chin.

"I am an old fool," he said at last. "But in my youth I loved your father well, and I love not my lord of Banworth. If I am caught and hanged it is no great matter after all, for in a very few years I shall have reached man's allotted span. Aye, I'll help you, Master Richard, if so be you have a plan."

"I have thought it all out!" said Richard eagerly. "When do you start for London, Crispin?"

"The day after tomorrow," Crispin told him. "Once m'lord and his men are out of the way, I shall prepare for the journey. They have left me naught but two pair of old horses and I must make shift, for all the best horses go to war. It will take me longer to get to London, but that is now of no importance since I shall never arrive."

"Why not?" asked Richard in surprise. Crispin gave a wry chuckle.

"If I help you to escape, then I must vanish also," he said. "Lady Eleanor is no fool and it will not take her long to

connect your disappearance with my departure. Riders will
be sent after us to bring you back, and a man on a fleet horse
will soon come up with my two pair of crocks. No, Master
Richard, London will not see me this time. We will leave the
wagon and horses at an inn, for steal them I dare not, and
you and I will journey to the forest on shanks' mare."

"You mean walk?" said Richard doubtfully. "Oh, how I
wish I could take Starlight with me!"

"Starlight goes to war," said Crispin shortly. "Did not
Master John tell you? He rides your palfrey when he sets out
tomorrow."

"It is not fair!" cried Richard passionately. "Why should
John have my horse?"

"There are other horses in the world," put in Odo quietly.
"It is your father of whom you should be thinking, not your
horse."

"I know," muttered Richard. "But all the same—" Then a
thought struck him and he said eagerly: "I must take Alys
with me!"

"*No!*" said Crispin. "No, Master Richard. That indeed
would be to put my head in the noose."

"I cannot go without her," said Richard stubbornly. "I
have given my word. A Travers does not go back on his word
to a lady."

"You will have us all hanged," groaned Crispin "Well, so
be it. The maid comes with us. But she must disguise herself
in boy's gear, for I will not be responsible for safeguarding
a young maid. The roads are infested with scoundrels, and a
maid could not slip by unnoticed like a poor old man and
a lad. She must cut her hair and wear a rough tunic and
hose. It is not seemly but it is safe."

"I had already thought of that," said Richard. "I had it all planned out. What we need are the clothes. Can you get rough gear for us, Crispin, for otherwise I know not how to come by it."

"Leave that to me," said Crispin resignedly. "Now listen carefully, Master Richard, for after tonight we had best not be seen talking together. I shall leave here before dawn. When the first faint light shows in the sky, you and the little maid must make your way to this place. How you manage this is your concern and I cannot help you. Hidden under the straw where that boy is sleeping you will find the gear. Change, and hide your own clothes in the straw. Daub your faces with mud and pull your hoods well down. Then join me in the outer bailey, where I shall be waiting with the wagon. I shall shout and swear at you and even strike you, Master Richard, for I am known to be short-tempered at daybreak and I must not give the guard any cause to suspect you are not what you seem. Walk at the wagon's tail as if dejected, and keep your heads low as we pass the guard. Once over the drawbridge and out of sight, you may both ride and we will make all speed we can, for we must be at the inn before the alarm is given. Put a cushion under your bedcovers and bid Mistress Alys do the same, so that to the casual glance it will seem you are both lie-abeds. It may give us a longer start."

"I shall be alone in Sir Hugo's room," Richard told him. "It may be quite late before anyone comes to see why I have not risen. Alys sleeps with the women, her task will be more difficult. And yet I think it likely that everyone will sleep later when the Baron is not here. John says everything becomes easier when m'lord has gone away."

"Very like," said Crispin. "It is a bold venture, but the Lord is on our side, or so I hope. Now be off with you,

Master Richard. It is late and you will be missed. Remember, do not approach me or speak to me until the time comes to leave."

"I'll remember," said Richard soberly. "Odo, what will you do? Will you come with us?"

"Nay," said the old man. "I shall stay here. Once the company has departed, my lady will be glad enough to welcome me into the hall and hear my songs and stories. But we shall meet again one day, perhaps in your own home. I wish you well, Master Richard. You are a brave lad, a worthy son of a noble father. One day I will weave your adventures into a song, and your journey of deliverance will be sung in halls all over the land."

Richard flushed with pleasure. To be the subject of a song and to have one's courage extolled, that were an honor indeed!

"The deliverance is not yet accomplished," put in Crispin dryly. "Be off with you, Master Richard, it grows late."

There was little sleep for anyone that night. Only for a couple of hours before dawn did quietness fall while exhausted men snatched a little rest. Richard slept fitfully and was awakened at first light by Sir Hugo, who laid a hand on his shoulder and whispered: "This is farewell, my little friend. Be a brave boy and do as you are bid."

"Oh, Sir Hugo!" exclaimed Richard, sitting up and brushing the hair out of his eyes. "I shall miss you so!"

"And I you," said Sir Hugo sadly. "But take courage. Perhaps this battle we shall fight may end the war and then you will be able to return to your home."

"I cannot wish you victory," said Richard. "But oh, Sir Hugo, I wish you safe!"

"Amen to that," said Sir Hugo with a sigh, and then he

was gone and the room seemed cold and lonely without him. Richard slipped out of bed, shivering in the chill of the dawn. He pulled the fur-lined bedcover around him and stationed himself at the window to watch the scene below. As he watched, the sun came up, tinting the castle walls with rose and gold, striking on the breastplates of the soldiers, and glinting off pikes and swords.

The horses were led out, tossing their heads and calling to those left behind. The heavy horses were harnessed to the baggage wagons, six horses to each. The knights' chargers followed, splendidly accoutered, and the rough, shaggy little horses of the Baron's serfs who had ridden in from their homes in the surrounding countryside the day before. With a pang Richard saw Starlight led out and held by a groom for John to mount. John's face was set and serious, all trace of childhood gone.

A trumpet blew and the men formed ranks. The Baron appeared outside the Great Hall, Lady Eleanor by his side. He kissed her hand ceremoniously and mounted his charger. The sun struck on him, turning his red beard to copper, glinting off the great jeweled brooch at his throat and on the sword belt around his waist. He gathered up the reins and, standing in the stirrups, looked around, then held up an arm in an agreed signal. Immediately the portcullis rose, the men, in a great upward surge of movement, mounted their horses and the wagon wheels began to turn. The Baron rode to the head of the cavalcade, his knights close behind, and as their horses' hooves drummed hollowly on the drawbridge, so the whole great company began to move. Trumpets sounded, banners waved in the fresh morning breeze, and Richard, with a lump in his throat, reflected that somewhere in that press of men rode Henry, homeward bound.

The riders swept on, over the drawbridge and away. The heavy wagons rumbled after them, a few last stragglers hastening behind. Then, suddenly, all were gone and the great castle stood empty and sunlit, silent and still.

10

Escape!

Richard woke before dawn on the day of the escape to the sound of heavy rain. It was cold in the stone-walled bed chamber, for since Sir Hugo's departure no fire had been kindled on the hearth, and in spite of the time of year the castle, without constant fires, soon became damp and chill. Richard curled himself into a ball under the coverlet and went over in his mind what he had to do.

"Watch the window," Crispin had said. The window faced east and the first hint of dawn would show as a faint grayness through the slit. Rise then, creep along the corridor and down the outside stair. He wondered if Alys too was awake and waiting for the moment of escape with a wildly beating heart like his own. If she should oversleep, or wake the women, there was nothing he could do to save her. He must go whether she came or not. He had given his word that he would not go without her, but since then a deeper loyalty had intervened, loyalty to his father. It would be a terrible thing if he had to leave Alys behind, but if she overslept there would be no choice.

A faint scratching came at the door and he started up, whispering: "Who is it?"

"Only me," a voice whispered back, and Alys slipped into the room.

"I could not sleep," she said breathlessly. "I was afraid that I might not wake in time and you would go without me. Oh, Richard, let us go now, before anyone is astir!"

"It is not yet dawn," said Richard doubtfully, but as he spoke, the sky outside the window lightened from black to gray and somewhere in the gardens a bird twittered sleepily. Then a cock crowed and Richard knew that dawn had come. He slipped from under the covers, and Alys saw he was fully dressed.

"Have you already been up?" she inquired, and Richard grinned.

"I slept in my clothes," he said. "There was no one here to ask questions." He picked up his table knife from a chest and thrust it into his belt. "This I shall want. We have to cut your hair."

"I wish we had not to cut it," said Alys mournfully. "It takes so long to grow, and I shall look very strange with hair only to my shoulders, like a boy."

"Bind it and wear a wimple," advised Richard, and Alys said crossly: "You know I cannot do that at my age. People would laugh at me."

"Well, it is no great matter," Richard told her impatiently. "But if you value your hair so much, do not come. Stay here and marry your French Count, although you will wear a wimple when you are married, no doubt."

"Now you are being unkind," said Alys reproachfully. "You know I want to come with you more than anything else in the world."

"Come then," said Richard. He opened the door cautiously and peered out. The long corridor lay dark, empty, and still.

Together they tiptoed to the outer door, slipped through, and ran down the steps in the rain. A dark shadow rose from under their feet, making them jump, but it was only a cat. From the Great Hall one of the wolfhounds barked sharply, and they froze where they stood, pressed up against the wall of the keep. No one stirred, but through the gloom and the driving rain they heard, from the outer bailey, Crispin's voice speaking gruffly to his team.

"He's there!" whispered Richard. "Quick! We must change our clothes. He will not want to wait."

The wagon shed was a welcome shelter from the wet. The gray light of dawn showed them the stack of straw, and when Richard burrowed into it, he soon discovered a bundle of rough clothing tied around with a leather thong. There were two pairs of coarse hose, two pairs of boots, two tunics such as the peasants wore, and two hooded, russet cloaks. They smelled strongly of horses, and Richard guessed that Crispin had stolen them from the sleeping stable boys. Alys wrinkled up her nose in disgust but said no word. She took up her bundle, retired behind the straw stack, and emerged as a spindling boy. She pulled her two long, fair plaits over her shoulders and whispered resignedly, "Cut them off."

Richard drew his knife and hacked at the plaits. They were harder to cut through than he had supposed. When the task was done, Alys's face was drawn with pain and tears stood in her eyes.

"Did it hurt?" asked Richard, and she said briefly, "A little. It is no matter. Do I look like a boy?"

"You are too clean," said Richard. Stooping, he rubbed his hands over the damp floor stained with axle grease and mud, then wiped them on his hair and face. "Now you," he said.

Alys shuddered, but did as she was told. Then she pulled

her hood well down over her shorn head. "Is that better?" she said.

Richard grinned.

"You look a very proper little peasant," he said. "And I?"

"A swineherd," Alys told him solemnly. "You have a great smudge on your nose."

"So much the better," said Richard. "Alys, are you ready? We must go."

It took courage to leave the sanctuary of the wagon shed and walk boldly across the bailey to where Crispin waited with the wagon. People were astir now; sleepy kitchen boys were carrying wood for the fires, a stable lad took buckets to the pump, and at the outer gate stood the guard. He was an old man, no longer fit to go to war, and he was leaning on his pike, talking to Crispin as the two children approached.

"So here you are at last!" shouted Crispin as he saw them appear. "Where have you been, you lazy, good-for-nothing pair?" Seizing Richard by the arm, he shook him, cuffed his ears, and thrust him toward the wagon.

"Keep your head down," he whispered. "Make believe to cry."

Richard sniveled and thrust his knuckles into his eyes, while Alys, startled by the old man's ferocity, burst into genuine sobs.

"Leave them alone, old friend," said the guard indulgently, "The lads are still half asleep, and no wonder. They seem little more than babes."

"And so they are," grunted Crispin with well-feigned disgust. "All the boys of any worth are gone with m'lord and I am left with the sweepings. I would do better to journey alone."

"The smaller one looks puny," said the guard. "Come here, lad, what is your name?"

"We have no time for idle chat," said Crispin hastily. "Open the gates. I must be on my way."

The guard shot a sympathetic look at Alys and gave her a kindly wink. Then he went into the gatehouse and the next moment the portcullis rose and, with a screaming of ratchets, the drawbridge spanned the moat. Crispin shouted at his team, urging them forward. The wheels turned, and as Richard and Alys stumbled hastily over the bridge at the wagon's tail, they heard the portcullis descend behind them. Castle Banworth was left behind!

Once out of sight of the castle, Crispin stopped the horses and said, "Up you get. From now on you ride, and I too, for we must make good speed."

Coming around behind the wagon, he lifted Alys and saw her comfortably settled on a pile of sacks. Richard swung himself up beside her. They were both muddy and wet and the rain lashed down mercilessly, but in spite of the discomfort their spirits rose, for at last they were free and on the open road. To the right of them the sea stretched out, gray and troubled by the wind; inland lay the downs, a sea of grass. The road was little more than a track, churned up by the feet of the great company of horses which had passed over it the day before, but the team made good speed with only an empty wagon to draw. Crispin rode sideways on the shaft and every now and again he turned and anxiously scanned the road behind them, but no hurrying horseman appeared, and their hopes grew with every passing mile.

They came to the inn after three hours' journeying. It was a small, humble little inn of mud and stone with its shaggy, thatched roof almost touching the ground at the back, like an untidy head of hair. A dog rushed out, barking savagely, and the dog was followed by a man, so wild and unkempt in appearance that Alys clasped Richard's hand and clung to him while her small face grew white. Crispin, however, greeted the man as a friend and asked his leave to stand the horses in his shed while he and his boys had a meal and rested for a while.

"We started before dawn," he said. "We are weary and have still a long way to go."

"Come you in," said the man. He looked indifferently at the two children as he helped Crispin to unharness the team. At a sign from the old man, Richard took one horse by the bridle and Alys, with great courage, took another. The huge horse tossed his head and nearly had her off her feet, but she clung on gamely, intent upon preserving her disguise.

"They give you babes for helpers now?" grunted the inn-keeper, and Crispin gave an exclamation of disgust.

"Two little conies!" he said bitterly. "More trouble than help, the pair of them. But I must needs make shift with what I can get. M'lord has ridden to Worcester to join Earl Simon, and every man and boy of any worth rides with him."

"More fighting," said the innkeeper. "So much for the de Montfort Parliament which was to right all wrongs and bring us peace. I would not say this to anyone but you, Crispin, my friend, but for my part I would like to see Prince Edward on the throne. De Montfort is, after all, a foreigner, and we English want no foreigners set over us."

"Many people are coming to think as you do," said Crispin soberly. "Maybe the Earl has had his day."

"Come you in and drink with me," said the innkeeper. "Your lads can keep watch over the horses. So much at least they can manage to do." He looked again at Alys and shook his head. "The scrapings of the barrel indeed," he said.

"What a horrid rude man!" exclaimed Alys indignantly when the two men had gone into the inn. "How dare he speak of me like that?"

Richard grinned. "He does not speak of Mistress Alys," he said. "He speaks of a stable boy, and you know you do look small and frail, Alys. Are you very tired?"

"Not very," said Alys bravely. "But oh, Richard, I am so hungry!"

"I wish I knew if Crispin had brought food," said Richard. "I am hungry too. But we had better do as we were bid and watch over the horses, or that man will suspect we are not what we seem."

"Even the horses are eating," sighed Alys as they went into the barn, where the four old horses were peacefully munching at a pile of hay. "Richard, do you suppose—"

"Listen!" said Richard suddenly. "I can hear someone coming along the road."

Seizing Alys by the arm, he pulled her down behind one of the horses. The sound of hoofbeats was coming nearer. They could hear the drumming on the road and the splash of mud as the unknown rider spurred his mount forward at a gallop. Nearer came the sound and nearer. Was it a messenger from the castle, come to find Crispin and bid him return? Had their absence been discovered so soon? It was still barely six o'clock and they had hoped for another hour of grace.

The hoofbeats were very close now, they were outside the inn. The rider would see the wagon—he must see it—for it stood in full sight. Any moment now, Richard thought desperately, the horse would stop, and after that it would only be a matter of minutes before they were discovered and hauled out and taken back to bondage. Great tears rolled down Alys's white face, and Richard set his teeth, looking around frantically for a way of escape from the barn, but the only door was in the front and there was no escape to be hoped for that way.

The hoofbeats were now so close they seemed to drum inside their heads. Then they were past, and dying away in the distance.

"He didn't stop!" gasped Richard. "Alys, he didn't stop! He wasn't looking for us at all!"

A figure cut off the light in the doorway and Crispin hurried into the barn.

"Are you there?" he said. "Lord, but that rider had me in a fright! I made sure he was after us."

"Me, too," said Richard. "Who was it, Crispin?"

"Nay, how should I know?" asked the old man testily.

"Some messenger in a hurry, no doubt. Some of these young men ride like demons, with no thought for their mounts. Still, the next traveler may well be the one we dread, and we must leave this place at once. I have told my friend that we wish to sleep for an hour and he will not disturb us. He is milking his cow at this moment, and his wife, idle woman, is still abed. Come, it is time we were gone."

"Crispin," said Richard hesitantly, "have you brought any food? Alys and I have not yet broken our fast."

"Nor me either," said Crispin. "I was too anxious before we started to have any stomach for food. But I have provisions in the wagon. Wait here while I fetch the bundle, and then we will be on our way."

He went out, looking cautiously around him as he left the shelter of the barn. The rain had stopped and a watery sun was rising and shining dimly through heavy banks of cloud. Birds twittered cheerfully in the thatch of the barn, and from somewhere close at hand came a great grunting of pigs.

In a moment Crispin returned with a bundle under his arm.

"Come," he whispered. "There is no one about, and we will gain the shelter of those woods before we stop to eat. Richard, take the little maid's hand and help her, for the going is rough."

On tiptoe, with beating hearts, the two children left the barn and followed Crispin down a muddy track which led to an oak wood. Pigs rootled for acorns under the trees, and a small boy in tattered clothing and long, unkempt hair, looked up at the travelers, startled, as they passed. Crispin paused, drew a coin from his pouch, and threw it to the boy.

"If you are asked, you saw us go *that* way," he said, pointing along a track to the right. The boy nodded, looking unbelievingly at the coin in his dirty hand.

"Let us hope he has wit enough to earn his money," said

Crispin uneasily. He led the way down the track which led
to the left, and they plunged into the dripping wetness of the
wood. In a very few minutes their heavy cloaks were almost
soaked through and their feet were so clogged with mud it
was difficult to put one before the other. Alys stumbled
along looking more dead than alive, but no word of complaint crossed her lips, and Richard regarded her with a new
respect. He was tired himself, and he was a boy and three
years older than she was. Often on hunting or hawking trips
he had experienced discomfort like this, but Alys was a little
girl, delicately raised. Probably she had never in her life
been out in the wet and certainly she knew nothing of mud.

He squeezed her hand and whispered: "Are you all right?"

Alys smiled bravely. "I am so very hungry," she said.

"Crispin!" called Richard, and the old man stopped and
said: "What ails ye?"

"Alys is weary. She must have rest and food," said
Richard, and his voice held a note of authority which the old
man was quick to recognize. Here, in spite of his small
stature and tender years, was a member of the ruling class.

He smiled grimly and yet approvingly as he answered:
"Take you the bundle, and I will carry the little maid.
Another furlong or so brings us out of this wood into open
country well away from any road, and there we will stop and
eat without the discomfort of wet from the trees dripping
down our necks. We will make a good meal then, I promise
you, for I helped myself from the kitchen this morning
before the cooks were about, and I have dainty food to
tempt a lady's appetite, as well as coarser fare for you and
me."

In another quarter of an hour they left the wood, Alys
riding upon Crispin's back. The mist was clearing fast and

there was some warmth in the sun. They were now in down-land country where huge flocks of sheep had nibbled the grass to a velvet fineness. Crispin set Alys gently down and spread out his cloak on a rocky outcrop.

"Sit you there," he said, "and eat."

Never, Richard thought, had food tasted so good! As his hunger disappeared, so his spirits rose. Crispin, too, seemed to cast off some at least of his anxiety, and Alys's eyes shone and her pale cheeks flushed pink as the fresh, upland breeze ruffled her shorn hair and the sun shone on her, making her wet clothes steam. When the meal was finished, she fell suddenly asleep, and the old man and the boy left her to rest while they discussed in low tones the route they should travel in order to find the hut in the forest where the Earl of Travers lay, a crippled fugitive, waiting for an uncertain deliverance.

11

At the Monastery

The day promised to be hot. By nine o'clock, when the travelers took the road again, the sun had dispelled the mist and shone brazenly out of a hard blue sky, making the sodden land steam like a pot on the boil.

Their way lay over downlands where sheep grazed and larks sang and the gorse smelled honey-sweet. Richard, refreshed by good food and rest, felt as if he could walk forever. The turf was springy under his feet and the upland air was fresh. Alys too seemed revived by her sleep and ran here and there, picking little bunches of the short-stemmed, downland flowers.

"A strange occupation for a boy," Crispin told her dryly. "It is well for us there is none to see you. Better that you should throw stones at the birds."

"Not all boys throw stones," expostulated Alys. "Richard does not."

"Master Richard flies his falcons at skylarks, I doubt not," said the old man. "It is in the nature of boys to be destructive, and it is in the nature of little maids to pick posies. I ask only that you remember that you are now a boy."

Alys sighed. "I will try," she said. "But the flowers are so pretty, it is hard to leave them alone."

"Let her be," said Richard. "Who is there to see?"

"There are shepherds on these downs," said Crispin crossly. "But if you think you know best, then take no heed of me. I advise you only for your own good, but no matter."

Richard exchanged glances with Alys and with difficulty restrained a laugh. Poor old Crispin was in the sulks! Then he looked at the old man's tired, anxious face, and remembering the terrible risk he ran in helping them to escape, he felt a prick of conscience.

"Throw down your flowers, Alys," he said sternly. "Thrust your hands into your belt and try to walk like a boy."

They walked, with frequent rests, until noon, when they ate again and slept in the shade of a small wood. Then on once more, weary now and footsore, until the sun began to dip behind the hills and they came at last to the gates of the monastery where Crispin had planned to spend the night.

"What a big place it is," said Alys in wonder as they drew near. "I had no idea a monastery was so big. What monks are they who live here, Crispin?"

"They are the Benedictines," said Crispin. "They have need of a big place, for they keep a hospital for the sick and a guesthouse for travelers like ourselves. More than a hundred monks live here. They cultivate the land and keep livestock and do all their own building, besides being men of God and very active about their prayers. Now, Master Richard, and you, Mistress Alys, you must not be affronted if we go to the most humble lodging. The monks have fine accommodation for the rich, but remember, you are now stable boys and must lodge with lowly folk. Be careful not to give yourselves away by any display of disgust if our fellow guests are dirty or foulmouthed. It is part of the price you must pay for your freedom."

"I care not what our fellow guests are like," said Richard. "And as for Alys, she is so sleepy she is past noticing anything."

"I am not!" said Alys indignantly. "I am as wide awake as you are, Richard. But Crispin, am I to lodge with the men?"

Crispin looked uncomfortable. "I fear so," he said. "It is not seemly, but then it is not seemly for a young maid of high birth to wander the roads clad in boy's gear. It is all unseemly, but there is no help for it since nothing would do but you must accompany us. I was against it from the first."

"Never mind," said Richard hastily. "We will find you a quiet corner, Alys, so don't be afraid."

"I think I would rather sleep under a tree," quavered Alys, but Crispin broke in, "So would not I! My rheumatics are too bad to allow me to lie in the open. Here at the monastery we shall find a dry bed and good food, and even if the guests are uncouth I prefer them to the company of badgers and hedgehogs. You must needs make the best of it, Mistress Alys, since you would come. Is it not enough for you that I am risking my neck, without giving me an attack of the ague into the bargain?"

"I am sorry," Alys murmured, but her small face took on the pinched look of anxiety which Richard was beginning to know so well, and he felt a flood of sympathy for her.

"I will protect you," he whispered. "Only remember at all times to play your part, for if anyone guesses you are a girl it might lead to our being caught."

Alys gave him a grateful look and took him by the hand. He shook her off hurriedly.

"There you go!" he said. "Have you no sense? When did you see two stable boys walking hand in hand?"

"Come along, come along!" called Crispin impatiently,

and they walked up to the gatehouse in silence. Here Crispin explained to the porter, an old monk, that he sought a night's lodging for himself and his two little grandsons.

"Come in, friend," said the monk kindly. "You look weary, all of you. Have you come far today?"

"We have come from Poole," said Crispin. "We journey to Winchester, where I shall leave these two youngsters in the care of my daughter, their aunt. Their mother and father have both died in recent months and I can no longer care for them."

"The poor little lads!" said the monk, and Richard felt a spasm of remorse that his pity should have been stirred by a lie. "It is sad to be orphaned so young, and the smaller one looks frail. Winchester is a great way off. Do you need alms, my friend? If so, go to the almonry and see Father Jocelyn and tell him your tale."

"Thank you, but we have no need for alms," said Richard proudly, and then realized his mistake as the monk looked at him in surprise.

"Hold your peace!" growled Crispin and cuffed him lightly over the head. "He is too saucy," he said in apology. "He lacks a father's hand."

"Pride is a bad fault in the young," said the monk disapprovingly, and saw them pass through the gateway without another word.

Once through the gate, they found themselves in a busy, bustling world. The courtyard was thronged with pilgrims, knights with their men-at-arms, merchants and traveling minstrels. There were many poor people too, travelers like themselves. The almoner was being kept busy in his small room just inside the gateway, dealing with numerous requests for aid. He was a stout, jolly monk with a red, smiling face, and had a cheery word to give to every supplicant, as well as small sums of money.

The lodging for poor folk lay to the left of the gate and that for richer travelers to the right. Across the courtyard lay the chapel and from the chapel came the sound of chanting, for it was six o'clock and Vespers was being sung. The abbot's lodging was next to the chapel, and stables and further lodgings for merchants and their kind made up the other sides of the great court. Behind the courtyard rose the roofs of many more buildings, and Richard caught a glimpse, through the cloisters, of large, well-laid-out gardens where lay brothers were working, their long habits hitched up around their waists and their bare feet thrust into leather sandals. A delicious smell of flowers wafted toward them on the evening breeze.

"I wish I could see the gardens," said Alys wistfully, and a monk who was passing by paused and smiled at her kindly.

"Do you love flowers, my little man?" he asked. "Then come with me, aye, and your brother too if he pleases. I will show you the gardens, and the abbot's carp who come to be fed when I ring a bell. And if you are good, who knows but that we might find a peach or a plum from the trees which grow against the walls."

"May we go?" asked Alys eagerly, and Crispin replied, "Aye, if you will, but have a care." He threw a meaning look at her and she nodded understandingly.

"I will—Grandfather!" she said and ran off happily, Richard following behind.

The monk led them through the cloisters, where they met a procession of brothers just coming from the chapel. It was their recreation hour and they walked up and down talking quietly together. Small rooms led off the cloisters; in one of them Richard saw a monk working with paints. He was illuminating a parchment with little pictures in brilliant colors, and when he looked up and caught Richard's eager stare he smiled and invited him in to see what he was doing.

"It is a Book of Hours," he said. "The King has ordered it as a present for his sister. Each page is to be decorated with little pictures and each capital letter is wrought in gold and scarlet with a device of flowers. Do you think it is pretty?"

"It is beautiful!" said Richard. "How clever you are!"

"My skill is a gift from God," said the monk. "I use my gift carefully, to the glory of the Lord. One day perhaps you may learn to read, my son, and then what a wonderful new world will open before you!"

Richard opened his mouth to say he could already read, and then shut it again hastily. It was he, and not Alys, who was in danger of forgetting his role!

The gardens were, in their way, as beautiful as the illuminated text. They were so neat, so colorful, that they looked almost unreal and like a painting themselves. Every plant, their guide told them, had its use, either for healing purposes or to flavor food or as strewing herbs, to keep the rooms sweet. Nothing was for beauty alone. "For to us use is beauty," he said.

"Roses are no use," argued Richard. "You have many roses here."

The monk smiled.

"From their petals we distil rose water, which is bought by fine ladies for their toilet, and the money they pay for it goes in alms to the poor. Moreover, roses feed the bees, and the bees give honey to sweeten our food, and wax for candles. Our very best chapel candles are made from beeswax. So you see, the roses are among the most useful of plants. But now, my little men, you must be longing for your supper, so back you go to your grandfather, who will be thinking I have spirited you away."

"It is so peaceful and nice here I wish we could stay forever," said Alys wistfully. "Sometimes I think I would like to be a nun."

Richard looked at her in horror, and her face crimsoned. Fortunately the monk had stopped to speak to one of the lay brothers and did not seem to have heard her remark. When he had finished his conversation, he put a hand on the shoulder of each and led them back to the courtyard, where Crispin was waiting for them. He had been given their rations for the evening meal, a kind of thick soup or stew made of vegetables and half a large loaf of bread. They sat down in the late afternoon sun to eat it and watch the comings and goings as they ate. Alys was very quiet; she knew Richard was upset with her for her indiscretion and she hoped he would not tell Crispin, who was cross enough already. But Richard too ate in silence, his head full of plans for what he should do when his father was found.

Suddenly the quiet of the evening was broken by the sound of tramping feet, and through the gateway rode a company of horsemen with, in their midst, a tall, handsome man on a chestnut palfrey. He was richly dressed in a bright blue tunic of wool with scarlet stockings and low boots of green. His belt and the brooch at his throat were set with jewels which flashed in the sun, and the linen coif on his head was embroidered in gay colors. In the somber courtyard of the monastery, among the crowd of humble people in drab clothes, he stood out like a peacock in a barnyard. But his face was set in cruel lines and he gave his orders in a loud, harsh voice, while his men scurried to obey. Presently

he dismounted and strode into the lodging reserved for the rich, while one of his men led his horse away and others busied themselves with unloading bundles of bedding and carrying them indoors.

Richard, turning eagerly to question Crispin as to who this fine nobleman could be, was surprised to see the old man crouched back in the shadow of the wall, his hood drawn well down over his face.

"Know you not who that is?" he inquired. "Mistress Alys, know you not that man?"

"I know him?" said Alys in surprise. "No, Crispin, of course I do not. Why should I know this strange lord?"

"Because," said Crispin soberly, "that lord is the Count of Clairembault, to whom you are betrothed."

12

Danger in the Night

Alys stared at Crispin in utter disbelief.

"The Count of Clairembault!" she exclaimed. "It cannot be! Why, Crispin, how do you know?"

"Five years ago," said Crispin, "when you were little more than a baby, he came to Castle Banworth to talk to your uncle about the marriage alliance. I saw him then and liked him not, and now I see him again I like him less. I would not give a dog to such a man, let alone a little maid."

"Do you think he is searching for Alys?" asked Richard anxiously. Crispin shook his head.

"Nay, how should he know that she has gone?" he said. "He is on his way to the castle, no doubt. It is a surprise visit, for I am sure the Countess knew nothing of it or great preparations would have been put in hand. The Count is rich, even richer than m'lord, and last time he came everyone in the castle was driven distracted by the entertainment prepared for him. No, he comes unheralded, of that we can be sure, and what he will say when he finds his future bride has vanished I do not care to think. Heads have been lost for less than this, and I would not care to be in your nurse's shoes, Mistress Alys, when inquiries are set afoot."

"What should we do?" asked Richard. "Do you think we should leave here tonight?"

The old man shook his head.

"I think not," he said. "We are as safe here as anywhere in the kingdom, for even if the Count knew of his bride's disappearance, which he does not, the last place he would seek her would be in the men's dormitory of a monastery, and the dormitory, moreover, given over for the use of the poor. There could not be a safer hiding place in all the world. But, Mistress Alys, guard your tongue and study your behavior, I beg you. One slip might lead to ruin for us all."

"I will be very careful, I promise you," said Alys soberly. "And, Crispin, I wonder that you call me Mistress Alys, even when we are alone. Someone might overhear. Call me—" she hesitated, seeking for a name, and Richard broke in: "Call her Nick, it is short and easy to remember. I will be Philip, and you may call me Pip."

"Nick and Pip!" said Alys delightedly. "It sounds just like two stable boys, does it not?"

"It matters not how you are called but how you behave," said Crispin repressively. "Nick, you eat too fine, supping your broth like a lady. And you, Pip, your look is too bold and will give you away. You should rather creep around, one arm up to ward off blows. Come you now to bed, for that is the safest place to be. We will make an early start tomorrow and be well on our way before the Count has even broken his fast. I confess I like not this development, for the search, which so far may have been halfhearted, will certainly become most serious once the Count arrives at the castle."

"But so few men are left behind," said Richard. "That at least is in our favor. Besides, how will they know where to look?"

"They will trace us to the inn," said Crispin. "After that, if the little swineherd does as I bid him, the trail will grow cold. And yet they may guess we would take shelter here tonight. We must rise early and make the best speed we can. Come to bed, and let us rest while we may. Oh, dearie me, that ever I was drawn into this desperate enterprise!"

That night they all three slept fitfully, and Alys was plagued by nightmares from which she woke screaming. Before the next day had fully dawned, the three fugitives were once more on their way.

"Why did you tell the brother that we were going to Winchester?" asked Richard after they had walked some way in silence, each busy with his own thoughts.

"First, because it was not true," said Crispin. "I did not like to lie to the good old monk, but I hope it is such a lie as will be forgiven me. Should inquiries be made for us, it is better for everybody that the monks know not the truth. Second, because Winchester is on the road to London and I know it well and could have spoken knowledgeably of my daughter's town if questions had been asked."

"Yes, I see," said Richard. "But which way do we really go?"

"We follow the London road as far as a village called Cadnam," Crispin told him. "That lies within the boundaries of the forest which they call hereabouts the New Forest. It is where—"

"I know!" Richard broke in. "It is the great hunting forest of King William the First. There it was that his son, William Rufus, was killed by an arrow—some say murdered. I have been to the spot where he was killed. My father took me and showed me a stone set up to mark the spot. Why, from there it is only about three hours' ride to my home!"

"True," said Crispin. "Three hours' ride on a swift horse,

but a much slower journey on foot. Still, we do not have to go so far, for the wood where your father is in hiding is this side of Travers Castle. Odo has described to me exactly which way to go."

"Do we have to travel through the forest?" asked Alys. "Oh, Crispin, will there be wild beasts?"

"Deer in plenty," said Crispin. "Wild boar too, but never fear, they will not harm us."

"Wolves?" quavered Alys. "Crispin, will there be wolves?"

"Nay, I think it very unlikely," said Crispin reassuringly. "In any case, we will travel through the forest in daylight, when the wild beasts are all asleep."

"I wish I had my bow," said Richard longingly. "I would dearly love to have a shot at a wolf."

Alys looked at him piteously, almost wishing herself back in the safety of Castle Banworth, but then she remembered the cruel, hard face and harsh voice of the Count of Clair-embault and decided that wolves were the lesser evil after all.

They traveled fifteen miles that day, resting frequently and eating the food the almoner had given them before they left the monastery. Dusk had fallen when they came at last to the little village of Cadnam on the edge of the New Forest. It was a very little village, consisting only of half a dozen mud cottages grouped around a green where a few lean goats grazed. The cottagers, Crispin said, lived chiefly by herding swine, great numbers of which ran in the forest, feeding on beech mast and acorns. The forest belonged to the Crown, and when the King or his sons wished to hunt there the cottagers were expected to drive the game—deer or wild boar—into the part of the forest where the huntsmen were gathered.

"They live in the midst of plenty," said Crispin. "But woe

betide the man who kills game to feed his hungry children. The penalty for poaching is death."

"I am glad I am not a poor man's son," said Richard soberly. "It seems the lot of the peasants is very hard."

"Are we to stay in one of those cottages tonight?" asked Alys, and as she spoke, a man came out of one of the low doorways and stood looking at them, a scowl on his face. He was clad in rags, his hair was long and unkempt. In his hand he clutched a stout cudgel, and at his heels a lean, mangy dog showed his teeth in a snarl. Alys gave a cry of terror and even Richard turned pale.

"Begone!" said the man, raising his cudgel over his head. "Get away! We want no strangers here!"

"We are poor, harmless travelers," said Crispin mildly. "We mean no ill, friend. All we seek is shelter for the night."

The man hesitated. Then a greedy light came into his eye and he said: "Can you pay?"

"Aye," said Crispin. "We have a little money. We can pay for a corner under your roof and maybe some goat's milk for the lads."

The man hesitated again, then he said: "Come you in."

The hovel consisted of one room with an earth floor and a fire in the middle of it. The smoke wreathed around and escaped through a hole in the roof. Chickens squawked and fluttered as the man kicked them roughly aside, then fled out of the door, leaving feathers and a rank smell behind. On a heap of dried fern in one corner a woman sat holding a baby in her arms, while two other small, pale children huddled close to her, peering fearfully at the strangers. A pot hung over the fire from a tripod, from which a smell of boiling turnips arose. Apart from this, the hut held nothing. It was the poorest habitation imaginable, and Richard drew in his breath and gave an exclamation of horror. Alys was looking at the baby, her face puckered up with pity and dismay.

"Good evening, mistress," said Crispin, but the woman only stared at him stupidly and held the baby more closely. One of the older children began to whimper, and his father dealt him a blow which sent him sprawling on the floor.

"We have lodgers for the night," he told his wife. "Get up and fetch more litter for the bed. Milk the goat and slice bread. This old gentleman has money and can pay."

"The goat is giving no milk now," said the woman faintly. "And we have no bread. There is nothing but a little turnip soup, barely enough for ourselves."

"It is no matter," said Crispin hastily. "We will not rob you and your children. We have some food left and will make shift with that."

"Must we stay here?" whispered Alys. "It is so dirty, Crispin, and there are no beds."

"It is a roof over our heads," said Crispin shortly. "It promises to rain before the night is over, and if I lie out in the rain I shall get an ague. I have told you that before."

Alys sighed, and said no more. The woman brought in an armful of dried fern and spread it on the floor, and the three travelers sat down and ate their bread and cheese, washing it down with water which the man brought to them in a cracked wooden bowl. Then they lay down to sleep and Crispin was soon snoring, but Alys and Richard lay awake, tormented by the fleas with which the hut was infested. At last, when the fire had died down to ash and the hut was pitch dark, they too slept, but an hour later Richard woke suddenly to the realization that somebody was moving stealthily around the hut. He lay very still, holding his breath, while his every instinct cried out that danger was afoot. As his eyes became accustomed to the darkness, he saw, in the faint glimmer of starlight through the hole in the roof, the figure of their host, and the star-shine glimmered on the blade of a knife he held in his hand. Softly he approached the spot where Crispin lay, the knife held high as he bent over the sleeping figure of the old man. With the courage of despair Richard sprang into action. Rolling over, he clutched the man around the legs and pulled with all his strength, at the same time yelling at the top of his voice. The man, taken off-balance, toppled forward and sprawled full length on the floor; the knife flew out of his hand and landed in the hot ashes of the fire. The children began to scream and in a moment there was pandemonium. In the darkness no one knew what had occurred, and when at last Crispin, with trembling hands, succeeded in kindling a light, the man had disappeared, and the woman, wild-eyed, crouched in her corner like an animal at bay.

"What is it? What happened?" demanded Crispin, and then his eye was caught by the glitter of the knife in the fire. "By Our Lady! The villain was after my purse!" he said.

"It was Richard who saved us!" said Alys, her eyes shining with admiration. "Oh, Richard, you are so brave!"

"I caught him around the legs," said Richard, his breath coming short. His own legs felt curiously weak and his heart was beating like a drum.

The woman in the corner gave a low cry. She crawled on her knees to Crispin and held up her clasped hands.

"Have mercy, sir!" she implored. "Oh, do not tell, or my husband will be hanged and the children will starve. He wouldn't have done it if times weren't so bad. Life is so hard, noble sir, for the likes of us! Please, sir, say you will not tell!"

"He tried to murder me," said Crispin sternly. "And I am no nobleman. I am poor, like yourselves."

The woman gave a short, bitter laugh.

"Poor like ourselves!" she exclaimed. "I'll wager you eat every day and have warm clothes to keep you from the cold. Look at those boys, and then look at mine! You would not know they belonged to the same race! If they were starving, would you not steal to fill their mouths?"

"The poor things!" said Alys. "Please, Crispin, I mean Grandfather, let the man go."

"Yes, let him go," said Richard. "After all, he did not steal your purse."

Crispin hesitated, then putting an arm around each, he turned them to the wall and spoke low.

"It is not a question of whether I show mercy, but whether the man returns again to the attack," he whispered. "An old man and two children are no match for a determined thief armed with a knife. In truth I know not what to do, for if we stay here we are penned in and at his mercy, while if we leave now, who knows where he may be lurking in the dark?"

"I do not think he will return," said Richard. "Let us pick up the knife, Crispin, and we will take it in turns to keep watch until daylight, you and I."

"But could we not give that poor woman some money?" asked Alys pitifully. "The children are so thin and pale, and the little baby—" Her voice broke in a sob, and Crispin said hastily: "Aye, she shall have a few groats. I cannot spare more, and I suppose neither of you have any money?"

"Not a groat," said Richard, and Alys shook her head.

"I did not know there were such wretched people in the world," she said miserably.

"There are many such," said Crispin. "The Lord created rich and poor, and the poor must bear their lot. Now, lie you down and sleep. I will keep watch."

"Call me in an hour," said Richard, stifling a yawn. "I will take my turn."

"We will see," said Crispin. He went over to the fire, raked the knife out of the hot ashes with a piece of stick, then picked it up held in a fold of his cloak. "Sleep," he repeated. "At dawn we will be on our way."

"May I hold your hand?" begged Alys in a whisper as they lay down on their pile of fern. "No one will see, and I am frightened, Richard. Please do not be cross."

Richard put out his hand and clasped hers reassuringly.

"You are safe with me," he said grandly. "Never fear, Alys, for we have the knife."

When they woke, the hut was empty save for themselves. The woman and her children had vanished, and of the man there was no trace. Crispin laid four groats in the bowl from which they had drunk, and after a moment's hesitation he laid down the knife by the side of it.

"In such poor circumstances a knife is of great value," he said. "I cannot bring myself to rob the man even though he would have robbed me."

"But suppose he is hiding among the trees?" quavered Alys. "Suppose he should attack you again?"

"I do not think he will," said Crispin. "The man had the courage of a trapped rat. Now he has had time to think what might be the terrible results of such a crime, he will be cooler. Besides, I believe his wife has joined him and she will counsel him wisely. Come, let us be on our way."

In spite of Crispin's words, it was not pleasant to leave the shelter of the hut and plunge into the darkness of the trees. Rain, as Crispin had predicted, had fallen heavily during the night, and the soft drip of moisture from the branches sounded like quiet footsteps before them, behind, and on either side. Little wild animals rustled among the bushes, and a badger, hurrying homeward in the dawn, grunted like a man clearing his throat. Crispin's pace grew faster and faster until Alys was running to keep up. When at last they were through the wood and out in open land, she threw herself face down on a patch of grass by the side of a stream and declared she could go no farther without rest and food.

The last of the bread from the monastery served for breakfast. It was now hard and dry, but they washed it down with sweet water from the little stream which flowed over pebbles and among water mints and rushes. When they had eaten, they bathed their feet, and went on their way refreshed.

"How much farther have we to go?" inquired Richard.

Crispin considered a moment and then said slowly: "Before the sun sinks tonight, you should be with your father once again."

13

The Charcoal Burners' Hut

The great hunting forest of King William the Conqueror stretched for miles in every direction, heavily timbered areas alternating with stretches of open country, gorse-clad and sandy underfoot. It was well watered with small, lazy streams running clear over pebbly beds, above which dragonflies hovered. Flowers grew in abundance, so that Crispin and Richard had a hard time to get Alys along. Wild life abounded, and although they saw no wolves or wild boar, there were deer in plenty. Squirrels chattered and scolded from the trees as the travelers passed below, and sandy banks were pitted with the burrows of conies.

Food was becoming a pressing urgency. Crispin's pouch was now empty, and as the day progressed, their hunger grew until the children at least could think of nothing else.

"Could we not catch a hedgehog and roast him in hot ashes?" suggested Richard. "One of my father's huntsmen told me how to do it. You cover the hedgehog in clay and—"

"First catch your hedgehog," said Crispin dryly. "In the meantime here is a patch of berries and we must make do with those."

Blackberries are good when they are juicy and ripe, but they are scarcely ripe in July and do not make a satisfying diet for people who have walked five miles on a breakfast of stale bread. As they set off again after the frugal meal, Alys's footsteps became slower and slower and old Crispin looked gray and spent. They stopped more frequently to rest, and when the sun began to travel down the sky, they were still several miles from the wood where, so Odo had said, stood the charcoal burners' hut.

Silently they plodded on, no longer taking any interest in the country through which they passed. Richard had a bad blister on his heel which made every step a torment, but he set his teeth and said nothing. He remembered his father telling him once when he had a toothache that courage was not only the bravery of the occasion but also the will to endure.

It was during one of their frequent rests that the sound of men's voices first came to them on the wind. The sounds were faint at first and far away but they were enough to make the fugitives forget their weariness in sudden fright. Men were shouting to one another, and then came the thunder of horses' hooves and the cracking of branches. Birds flew up out of the trees in alarm, and a fox suddenly appeared, belly to ground, and slipped silently into the shadows of the wood.

"Huntsmen?" queried Richard, and Crispin said uneasily, "Aye, but what do they hunt? Is it fox or deer, wild boar or—you and I?"

As he spoke, they heard, above all other noises, the baying of hounds. Then a horseman appeared for a fleeting second between the trees, and Richard saw with horror that he wore the livery of the red Baron!

He turned to Crispin and saw the old man's face had turned gray.

"It is all up with us," said Crispin quietly. "It is bitter that we should be taken when we are so near the end of our journey."

"But we shall not be taken!" cried Richard urgently. "Come, quick! Let us hide in the wood!"

"The hounds will track us down," said Crispin resignedly. "It is useless, Master Richard. We cannot escape the hounds."

"We must and we shall!" said Richard. "Alys, you would not give up and be captured, would you?"

"Never!" said Alys. "I—I would rather die!"

"It is I who will die, not you," muttered Crispin. He seemed to have lost all hope, all power to think or move. Richard pulled urgently at his arm.

"We will hide in a tree!" he exclaimed. "The hounds may not find us there."

The bushes rustled violently and parted, and two huge hounds appeared. They looked at the little group before them with bright, dark eyes, but they did not bark. Instead they waved their long tails and stood panting, red tongues lolling out of the sides of their mouths.

"Shamus! Tara!" whispered Richard, and the great hounds dropped their ears and trotted to his side. Richard threw his arms around Tara's neck and kissed Shamus on the nose.

"Oh, my beauties," he whispered. "Did they think they could set you to hunt us down?"

"Can you make them go away, Richard?" asked Alys in a trembling voice. "Oh, do try, quickly, for I can hear horses' feet!"

Richard let go the dogs, stood up, and pointed.

"Home, Shamus!" he commanded. "Home, Tara!"

The two hounds gave him a surprised look, then turned

obediently and trotted away. The sound of voices and hoof-beats grew faint in the distance, and silence flowed back into the wood.

Richard found he was shaking all over. He sat down rather suddenly on a fallen tree and gave a tremulous laugh.

"They will follow the hounds for many miles before they discover they are on their way home," he said. "How glad I am that I made such friends with them. My father always said I had great power over animals, and I begin to think he was right."

"You are wonderful!" said Alys, the admiring look coming once more into her face, and even Crispin allowed unwilling, "It was well done."

The reprieve seemed to give them all new life. They set off again almost briskly but had not gone far when they heard the loud creaking of wheels and drew back into the bushes in alarm.

Along a track between the trees came a very old horse drawing a very old cart, the ungreased wheels of which screamed like a frightened pig. A very old man walked beside the cart, and a gray-muzzled dog followed slowly at his heels. The cart was piled high with a late cut of hay. The old man looked so harmless that Richard made a sudden resolve to ask his aid, and as the cavalcade passed their hiding place, he stepped out on to the track and held up his hand. The horse stopped without being bid and the old man looked up blearily and said, in such thick country tones that Richard could hardly understand him: "What do ye want of me?"

"My grandfather and my little brother are weary and we have still some way to go," Richard told him. "If you will let them ride in your cart, we will give you a groat."

"Where would ye go?" queried the old man, and Crispin said: "Know you a hamlet called Bramshaw?"

"I should know it," grunted the old man. "For it is there that I live."

"Take us thus far and you shall have your groat," said Richard.

"For two groats you may all ride," said the old man. "You are limping, boy, and there is blood coming through your shoe."

"I will give him two groats," said Crispin. He lifted Alys into the cart. "Up you get, Pip. Do you think I have not noticed that you are as lame as a duck?"

It was bliss to lie on the soft hay, to look up at the sky through the branches, and to listen to the monotonous clop-clop of the ancient horse's feet. Crispin fell almost at once into a doze, Alys nodded wearily, but Richard felt wide awake and his excitement grew with every mile as they drew nearer and nearer to the end of their journey. How would his father look? What would he say? Would he be pleased that Richard had escaped, or would he think he should have stayed safely at Castle Banworth until the war was over? And Alys—what would he think of her? For the first time Richard reflected on the seriousness of having stolen an heiress, and one moreover betrothed to a rich and powerful man, from her legal guardian's care. His father, lying crippled and helpless, might well think Richard had only added to his troubles by such a bold action. Suppose he said Alys must go back? Richard turned his head and looked uncertainly at Alys's little, weary face with its fringe of raggedly cut, corn-colored hair. She looked babyish and most unlike a rich nobleman's future bride. The thought of her in the power of the hard-faced man they had seen at the monastery made Richard feel weak with pity. Even in three years' time, when she was judged old enough to marry, she would be only twelve. It was very young to go alone save for one's servants to a foreign country and a new life.

It was the King who had given the red Baron the wardship of Alys. He must have done it before this war started, when he and the Baron were still friends, for it was a mark of the King's favor to give well-to-do orphans into the care of his friends. Rich rewards went with them and such guardianships were eagerly sought. Now the King and Baron Banworth were enemies, so what more likely than that King Henry would favorably receive Earl Travers's request that he should become Alys's guardian in place of the treacherous Baron?

Richard's hopes rose, and nudging Alys in the ribs, he whispered: "Would you like it if my father were made your guardian?"

"Oh, I would!" Alys whispered back with such longing in her voice that Richard felt noble at having thought of such a scheme. But then Alys spoiled it all by continuing: "And then, later on when I am older, I could marry you, Richard, instead of the French count."

"No, thank you," said Richard hastily. "I do not mean to be unkind, Alys, but I have no thought of marriage yet. You shall be my sister."

"But you have a sister already," said Alys dolefully.

"Why, so I have!" said Richard. "It is hard to remember about her, she was so very young when I left. But one can have two sisters, Alys, and you will be my favorite because of the adventures we are going through together."

"Oh, Richard," Alys whispered, her face very white. "Suppose I am obliged to go back to my aunt and uncle? What will they do to me for running away?"

"You shall not go back," said Richard stoutly. "We will have the King on our side. He loves not the French, and I daresay he hates the Count of Clairembault."

"But the King is almost the prisoner of Earl Simon de Montfort," said Alys. "And he is French, so perhaps he will not let the King take our side."

Richard did not know what to say to this, but fortunately at that moment the cart stopped and Crispin said: "Here we get down. Thank you, my friend, for your timely help. We have not much farther now to go"

He fumbled among his clothes and produced his purse, thin now and all but empty. The man took his money eagerly and then, without speaking, slapped the old horse on the flank and clopped off into the dusk.

"Have we really not far to go?" inquired Richard. "Do you know the way?"

"Aye," said Crispin. "Odo gave me careful directions and we have had luck, for the cart has brought us to the very spot where we are to leave the road. That wood there is the one where your father is in hiding."

He pointed, as he spoke, to a stretch of forest where the trees pressed so close together that beneath them it was almost perpetual night. Wood doves cooed in the branches and a great white owl flew out on silent wings, making them start, it came so low. The undergrowth looked impenetrable and there were no paths to be seen.

Crispin glanced up at the sky.

"The clearing where the hut stands lies to the west," he said. "Our way is marked for us by the setting sun."

"It will be rough going," said Richard, looking at the tangle of briars. He drew the knife from his belt and went on. "I will lead the way."

"Mistress Alys had better bring up the rear," said Crispin.

"In that way we shall tread out a path for her to follow."

"Oh no, please!" cried Alys, and as the other two looked at her in surprise, she said lamely, "If a wolf should come up from behind—"

Crispin smiled grimly and stood back to let her pass. "Better, you think, that old Crispin should make a wolf's supper—" he began and Alys said remorsefully, "No, no, dear Crispin, I was not thinking! Of course I will go last!"

"There are no wolves," said Richard impatiently. "All the same, Alys had better walk between us two, in case she falls, or is struck by a branch. Only let us start! It will be dark soon and if we lose ourselves we may go around in circles all night."

At first the going was so difficult that Richard almost despaired of ever getting through. The wood had, over the years, girded itself around with a barricade of hazel bushes, blackberry vines, and bracken the stems of which were as thick as a man's riding whip. Whichever way the charcoal burners had come and gone to their hut, it had not been this way, or else the hut had been abandoned for many years. By the time the travelers had gone fifty yards, they were exhausted, and scratched beyond belief. Blood stained their faces from the attacks of the vicious, tearing thorns, and Richard had a red weal across his forehead where a branch had whipped back and knocked him to the ground. Alys stumbled on, more dead than alive, her yellow hair full of twigs, her clothes torn and stained. Crispin too was near the end of his tether when suddenly they came upon a narrow path, a mere deer track, but wide enough for a man to pass unscathed. Presently the track widened and for the first time they saw the sky, red from the sunset, through the tall, interlacing trees. The track ran on, twisting and turning, and

they followed it eagerly, their tiredness and pain forgotten.

Suddenly Richard stopped short. A little stream, scarcely more than a trickle, crossed the track, and in the soft ground by its side showed plainly the mark of a man's shoe!

"We are getting near," said Richard in a voice that trembled a little. "Gregory must have been this way."

Everything was very still with the hush that comes on the earth before the death of the day. Nothing moved in the forest, no bird twittered, no wind stirred the leaves. Although the three walked softly, their footsteps sounded loud, and their hearts beat fast. Suppose it was not the faithful Gregory's foot which had made the mark by the stream? Suppose that since Odo had been there, enemies had come to that hiding place and taken both man and master away? There could be no knowing what to expect until they reached the hut, and no way of finding out except to go forward. Richard's hands felt clammy and he wiped them surreptitiously on his cloak. Alys prayed under her breath, and old Crispin's face was grim.

The smell of wood smoke told them they had reached their goal, even before they saw the hut. The smell was homey and good and gave them courage. They turned the last bend in the winding path and came out into the clearing just as the last rays of the sun struck on it, turning the rough thatch of the little hut to gold. A thread of blue smoke went straight up from a hole in the roof and with it came the smell of boiling meat, a savory, heartening smell. A rumble of voices came from within the hut and then the low doorway was darkened by the figure of a man. He stood upright, looking at the sky, and then, as his eye fell on the three travelers, he gave a great start and his hand flew to the knife at his belt.

"Gregory!" cried Richard, and running across the smooth turf before the hut, he flung himself against the tall man, clutching him by the arms and rubbing his head against the leather jerkin in an ecstasy of delight.

"By Our Lady!" exclaimed the man. "Master Richard, is it really you?"

"Who is it?" called a voice from inside the hut. "Gregory, who is there?"

"It is your son, m'lord!" cried Gregory in a great voice, and Richard left him and went into the hut alone.

14

In the Name of Friendship

"A council of war," said Lord Travers, looking around at the little company. "Gregory, my good man, I want you, yes, and you, Crispin, and Richard."

"You do not want me?" asked Alys rather forlornly. The Earl smiled.

"Certainly I want you, my little maid," he said kindly. "A woman has ever a ready wit. We cannot do without you."

It was the following morning, a beautiful, fine July morning with a heat haze hanging over the trees. The wood doves cooed drowsily, and the little forest clearing seemed like the quiet heart of the world.

The Earl lay outside the hut on a bed improvised by the resourceful Gregory from poles and the skins of deer. His legs were useless, paralyzed by the cruel blow from the battle-axe, but thanks to the care of his faithful body servant, he had kept in fair health, and his brain was keen and active. Crispin still looked tired and he complained of the ache in his limbs, but Richard and Alys, after a wonderful supper of venison stew and a good night's rest, felt fit for anything that might come.

Richard's father had taken the news about Alys with his usual calm. He had smiled a little ruefully when Richard

told him of her escape, and looked thoughtful at the mention of the Count of Clairembault.

"I have met him at the French court," he said thoughtfully. "He has a reputation for ruthless cruelty to his peasants. There are ugly stories told of him in France. I do not think he is a fit husband for your little friend. But what to do—that is our problem."

"We must not let the Baron get her back," Richard said anxiously. "She wants you to be her guardian, Father. Can you not petition the King?"

"The King is at present at Worcester in an uneasy alliance with the Earl of Leicester," said Lord Travers. "That, at least, is what Odo told us on his recent visit."

"But have you not heard of Prince Edward's escape?" cried Richard. "He is gathering his forces and will march against the Earl!"

"No!" exclaimed his father, raising himself up and looking at Richard eagerly. "You are sure of that?"

"Quite sure," said Richard. "Simon de Montfort sent to the Baron to come quickly and bring reinforcements and he started the day before we escaped. By now he should be with Earl Simon and perhaps they are already doing battle with the Prince."

"God grant the foreign usurper be defeated," said his father quietly. "He could have been a great man, but he has become drunk with power, and power corrupts all men. England would be well rid of him now. King Henry is weak, but he grows old and soon Prince Edward will be our sovereign lord. I have much faith in that young man."

"Do you think he will win the battle against Earl Simon?" asked Richard, and his father smiled.

"Nay, how can I tell?" he said. "I know nothing of his resources or the disposition of his troops. For months I have led the life of a hermit, starved for news. Odo is the only man who has come near me since I left our home. He at least brought me tidings of your mother and the babe. But now that you are here, and old Crispin, we can make plans."

That had been last night, before they lay down to rest. Now the plans were to be made. Richard felt a tremor of excitement. Whatever the future held, it would be better, far better, than being a prisoner at Banworth Castle. It might still be a weary while before he saw his home again, but at least he was free and united with his father and that, for the present, was enough. He waited eagerly to hear his father speak.

"Our main objective," said Lord Travers, "is to gain possession of my castle. Odo tells me there is only a small garrison left in charge, and of that garrison it may well be that some men have been drawn off to join the Earl of Leicester's army at Worcester. Now! About ten miles from here, to the north, lies the manor of my old friend Sir Peter Harcourt, your godfather, Richard."

"I remember him well," said Richard. "He visited us when I was very small and gave me a knife, which my mother would not let me have."

"I am glad you remember him," said his father. "For it is to him that I wish you to go."

"Alone?" asked Richard, hoping he did not show the anxiety that he felt.

The Earl smiled. "Gregory shall accompany you," he said. "I have long wished him to go and seek aid, but he would not leave me. For the first time since he has been in my service, he refused to obey my orders."

"I could not leave your lordship," said Gregory reproachfully. "Your lordship knows I am your obedient servant, but to leave you alone in this wilderness, helpless as you are, I could not deem to be my duty."

"I think Gregory was right," said Richard. "Far better that he should stay and tend you."

"Well, now he is free to go," said Lord Travers, looking affectionately at his faithful servant. "I shall be in good hands with Crispin here and the little maid."

Alys crept to the side of his bed and timidly clasped his hand.

"I will be a daughter to you," she whispered. "Only do not send me back."

"Of course he will not send you back!" cried Richard, and his father gave him a quizzical look.

"I am in no case to send anyone anywhere," he said. "Save

you, Richard, and you I send for aid. Mistress Alys stays with me for the present, though this is no fine lady's bower. If and when we regain our home, we will see what can be done. Who knows how our fortunes may run in the next few days or weeks?"

"When shall I start?" asked Richard, and his father said: "Tomorrow, when you are rested. It should not take you much above three hours to cover ten miles, but you must proceed with caution, for we know little of the state of the country and I would not have you and Gregory fall into the hands of the enemy and be lost to us once more."

The rest of the day was spent in preparations for leaving the invalid and his new attendants alone. Gregory, taking Richard aside, confided his fears that their mission might end in failure and that they might be captured by hostile forces. If that should happen, the three people at the hut would be in sore straits.

"A cripple, an old man, and a little maid," said Gregory. "What a trio to leave to their own devices in the midst of a forest!"

"I wish my father would agree to my going alone," said Richard, with a show of courage he did not really feel. "In that way if—if I were captured, my father would at least be no worse off than he was before."

"Nay, but he will not consent," said Gregory. "It is too hazardous a journey for a young boy to make alone, there I agree with my master. We must just do what we can to insure that they survive if we—if we are away longer than—"

"If we do not return," Richard finished for him. "What should we do, Gregory? You know I will help you all I can."

"Then you and Crispin gather fuel," said Gregory. "Even Mistress Alys can help by picking up sticks for kindling. I will go hunting and try to get a stag. I will show Crispin the best places to set traps for conies too, that they may have a change of meat. Then we will bring water, enough to last them for two days at least. More than this we cannot do."

"They cannot live on meat alone," protested Richard. "Have you no flour for bread?"

"A little," said Gregory. "I bought a sack of barley meal from a farmer, but he asked too many questions and I dare not go near him again. In any case, he is a poor man and has not much to sell. I will teach Mistress Alys how to bake flat cakes on a hot stone, and how to make a drink with mint from the brook, bruised and boiled in water. Your father finds this refreshing, in the absence of sack or wine. Then I must instruct Crispin how to lift my master and how to rub his back to ease the cramps. M'lord suffers greatly, Master Richard, but not one word of complaint has ever passed his lips. He is a great gentleman and his courage is an example to us all."

"High courage," murmured Richard to himself, and prayed that he too might show courage on his mission and be worthy of his father's trust.

They left at daybreak while Alys and Crispin still slept. The Earl was awake to give them their final instructions and a signet ring on which was engraved the Travers crest.

"Take this, my son," he said, holding it out to Richard, who took it and placed it carefully in the pouch on his belt. "Give that to Sir Peter as proof that you do indeed come from me. Gregory he may not remember, and you he could scarcely recognize, seeing you were but five years old when you last met. Tell him the whole story of my escape and your captivity, and convince him, if you can, that now is the time to make a bid to recapture Travers Castle for me, and for the

King. When he hears that m'lord of Banworth with all his
followers has set out for Worcester, I think he will agree the
time has come to strike."

He looked uncertainly at the small boy standing before
him and went on doubtfully, "Perhaps I should not let you
go."

"I am willing to go alone, m'lord," put in Gregory, but
Richard cried, "No! It is for me to go, sir! We are demanding
a favor of Sir Peter and it is more fitting that the request
should come from your son. I can speak to him as an equal,
which Gregory cannot."

The Earl of Travers smiled, but it was a proud smile.

"You are right," he said. "Furthermore, if Sir Peter agrees
to our request, it would be fitting if you stayed to ride with
him to fight for our home. Let Gregory return here, but do
you stay and fight."

"M'lord—!" protested Gregory, and stopped at a look from
his master.

"It is my wish," said the Earl quietly. "If I were not
crippled, I would ride with Sir Peter and fight by his side. As
it is, I send my son."

"I will try to do my duty, sir," said Richard in a low voice,
and then he and Gregory went out of the hut and into the
early morning quiet of the great forest.

The path they took was very different from the path by
which the travelers had entered the wood two days before.
It was narrow and winding but clearly defined and free from
thorns. Presently it joined a wide, grassy ride, and Gregory
told Richard that huntsmen sometimes came that way. The
ride ran on until they reached the northern boundary of the
forest, when they found themselves in country which Richard recognized as similar to that which lay to the south.

Presently the land began to rise, and they clambered up a hill thick with bracken. By the time they reached the top, they were hot and breathless, for the sun was now scorching down out of a hard blue sky. There was no shade and the flies were a torment to them both.

"How much farther have we to go?" inquired Richard, and Gregory gazed around him and then pointed. Richard, following the line of his finger, saw in the distance a belt of tall trees and, spiraling up from behind them, the blue smoke of a fire.

"The manor lies behind those trees," said Gregory. "It is not above another two miles. But from now on we must be on our guard, for the country becomes populated. There are farms and cottages belonging to the Manor, and although Sir Peter is for the King, we know not what forces of the enemy there may be in the district. In these days when brother is set against brother and England is split in twain, one must regard every man as an enemy until he proves himself a friend."

"Suppose the Manor is also in the hands of de Montfort's men, as our castle is?" said Richard. "What then?"

"We believe that to be unlikely," said Gregory reassuringly. "The Manor is of no strategic importance. It is little more than a large farm, though it has a moat and at one time may have been fortified, or so I hear. I have never been there myself. Sir Peter is peace-loving and lives only for the chase. He has a notable pack of hounds, famous all through the country."

"He does not sound the sort of man who will want to go to war," said Richard doubtfully. "Has he no soldiers about the place?"

"He has his tenants," said Gregory. "I daresay he can

muster at least a hundred men. They will arm themselves with staves and pikes and hunting knives and they will follow wherever Sir Peter leads. Have no fear, Master Richard, if Sir Peter is a free man, he and his will come to our aid."

They descended the far side of the hill and found themselves on tilled ground. A small house lay to the left with cattle grazing nearby.

"One of Sir Peter's outlying farms," said Gregory. "We will give it a wide berth since we still do not know what circumstances prevail."

They skirted the farm cautiously, seeing no one, and had gone another mile before coming upon any other signs of life. This time it was a cottage where a very old woman sat in the doorway spinning wool. She raised her head as they passed, but they saw with pity that her eyes were sightless.

Suddenly Gregory stopped short and, putting a hand on Richard's shoulder, drew him to the shelter of a bush.

"Listen!" he said, and Richard held his breath.

The baying of hounds came to them, bell-like and clear. They were running toward the cottage, and with every second the baying became louder, and soon it was joined by the drumming of horses' feet. A stag burst out of the undergrowth and passed them, its eyes wide and frightened, its feet pounding the earth. Then came a great wave of hounds in full cry, and behind them horsemen, riding hard. At the very rear was a stout, red-faced, jolly-looking man on a sturdy, weight-carrying horse. He had lost his head covering in the chase and his long gray hair streamed in the wind.

"It is Sir Peter!" exclaimed Gregory, and Richard, without stopping to think, ran out in the path of the rider, waving his arms. The horse shied and reared and its rider bellowed with rage as he fought to get his mount under control. When at last he succeeded in doing so, the rest of the hunt had disappeared into the distance and the belling of hounds came faintly on the breeze.

Sir Peter glared at Richard, his fat, kindly face wearing an unaccustomed look of rage.

"Are you mad, boy?" he exclaimed. "Your foolery all but had me off my horse!"

"I ask your pardon," said Richard. "I acted without thinking. I was so very anxious to stop you—Godfather."

"Hey?" exclaimed Sir Peter. "Godfather? Why, what is this? Who are you?"

"I am Richard Travers, your godson. I come to you from my father," said Richard.

"Your father?" repeated Sir Peter incredulously. "Now I know you must be lying, boy. The Earl of Travers is dead."

"Not so, sir," said Gregory, coming to Richard's aid. "M'lord lives, but he is crippled and in hiding. Master Richard comes to you in his place to ask for your help."

Sir Peter stared at them both in utter astonishment. Then he said slowly, "What proof have I that this tale of yours is true?"

Richard felt in his pouch and found the ring. He held it out to Sir Peter on the palm of his hand.

"The proof is here, sir," he said. "And in my face, if you look close, for people say I am very like my father."

Slowly, Sir Peter dismounted from his horse. He handed the reins to Gregory, and laying a finger under Richard's chin, he turned his face to the light.

"Aye," he said, and smiled for the first time. "Aye, Godson, the proof is in your face, as you say. And so your father lives? That is the best news I have heard since this tedious war began. There is nothing that interferes with a man's sport so much as war. Still, from what I hear the country may soon be rid of this tiresome foreigner who has stirred up so much trouble."

"You mean Lord Simon de Montfort?" inquired Richard eagerly. "Why, sir, what have you heard?"

"News came through yesterday that Prince Edward has taken Kenilworth Castle," said Sir Peter with great satisfaction. "That is a notable victory and must have been a sore blow to m'lord of Leicester. But now, Godson, what has your father to ask of me?"

"He asks you, in the name of friendship," said Richard slowly, "to march with me on Travers Castle and help me to free our home."

15

The Secret Passage

For a moment Sir Peter Harcourt looked at the small figure before him in silence. His eyes twinkled and his face grew redder than before, but he did not laugh. Instead he laid a hand gently on Richard's shoulder and said: "I shall feel honored, Godson, to be your brother-in-arms. Have you any knowledge of how the castle is defended, for to be forewarned is to be forearmed?"

It was Gregory who answered his question.

"News has reached us through Odo, the minstrel, sir. He spent a night in the castle recently and reports that the garrison there is small, not above twenty men. But even twenty men may hold attacking forces at bay when the drawbridge is up and the portcullis is down. The breach in the walls has been repaired, and without siege engines and strong forces I know not how we shall make our way in."

"Hmm," said Sir Peter thoughtfully. "We have a problem before us. Only twenty men, say you? My stout fellows would soon dispatch twenty men if only they could come at them. But twenty men snug and safe behind the curtain wall, that is quite another pair of shoes. We must think, but before we think you must rest and eat." He sighed. "The hunt is over for me, for this day at least. Let us go home, and my wife will find you food and make a rare fuss over this young warrior, I'll be bound. Up on the saddle behind me, boy!"

As he spoke, Sir Peter heaved himself on to his patient horse once more, and Gregory helped Richard up behind him. Then, with Gregory holding the stirrup leather and running beside the horse, they all made their way back to the Manor. Here Lady Harcourt, as plump and as jolly as her husband, made them welcome. Gregory was sent to the servants' quarters and entertained royally on such food and drink as he had not seen for many months, and Richard was petted and cosseted and made to tell every detail of his and his father's adventures since Travers Castle fell to the enemy.

It was while he was telling of his father's escape that the great idea suddenly struck him and he stopped talking so abruptly that Lady Harcourt said anxiously: "Why, what ails the child? Have you come over faint?"

"No, I'm quite well," said Richard. "But, oh, Sir Peter, I have just had such a splendid idea! I know how we can get into the castle without breaching the walls! We will steal in at night and under cover of the darkness take the enemy by surprise."

"Would you call witchcraft to your aid?" demanded Sir Peter, but his wife, quicker-witted, exclaimed, "The tunnel! The tunnel, of which Richard has just told us!"

"Yes, the tunnel!" said Richard excitedly. "If my father and Gregory could pass through it, so can we!"

"That is a matter for some doubt," said Sir Peter, looking ruefully at his large stomach, which almost rested upon the table as he sat at the head of it in his high-backed chair. "What size is this passage or tunnel and where does it start and end?"

"The castle entrance is under a mock tombstone in the chapel," Richard told him. "The entrance outside the castle is, so Gregory says, in the midst of thick shrubs about fifty yards beyond the curtain wall."

"One thing puzzles me," said Sir Peter. "If your father knew of this passage, why did he not use it early in the siege to send a messenger for help?"

"He could not," said Richard. "The exit was in the midst of the enemy camp. It was not until they breached the walls and the troops poured into the bailey that the land around the castle was left unguarded and so he and Gregory were able to escape. I asked my father that same question. But now that all the enemy are within the walls, there will be no one to see us enter the passage! Imagine their surprise when we pour out of the chapel and set upon them in the night!"

"Mercy me, it sounds very dangerous," sighed Lady Harcourt. "Richard, you will remain here in safety until the castle is won."

Richard looked at her in horror. Stay safely at the Manor like a child and miss all the excitement? Surely she could not make him do this thing!

"My father said I was to accompany Sir Peter," he stammered. "It was his special wish."

"The boy shall go," said Sir Peter, and Richard turned to him with a sigh of relief. "He is a brave boy and a good boy and will not foolishly run into danger, knowing, as he does, how dependent his father will be on him in the future."

"How soon can we start, sir?" asked Richard eagerly, and Sir Peter said, "It will take me some days to rally my men and see that all are properly armed. I fear our pikes are blunt and rusted, for we are peaceful here and not attuned to war. Then I had rather wait a little till the moon is on the wane, for surprise is our strongest weapon, and we need the darkness for that. How say you, Godson, if we venture forth a week from today?"

"So long?" cried Richard in dismay. "But my father and Alys and Crispin can never manage alone for so long."

"We will send Gregory back to them with provisions," said Sir Peter. "A week is not so very long."

"Can we not bring them all here?" asked Lady Harcourt, but Sir Peter shook his head.

"Better they should stay where they are," he said. "Not every man in this part of the country is our friend, and if they should be seen, it would start rumors and speculation and the garrison at the castle might be put on their guard. No, they must play at hermits just a little longer."

"Then I will go and put up food and comforts for them," said Lady Harcourt and went briskly away.

"Shall I go back with Gregory?" asked Richard, but again Sir Peter shook his head.

"Stay here and keep out of sight," he said. "Gregory will travel quicker alone, and your father's mind will be more peaceful if you remain safe in my care. But Gregory must return to guide us to the tunnel, and no doubt the brave fellow will wish to be in the forefront to strike a blow at the enemy."

"So will I," said Richard, but with little hope. He knew that Sir Peter would do all he could to keep him out of the fighting. Nevertheless, next day he took his knife to the grindstone, where an old servant was busy putting an edge on axes, pikes, and daggers, and persuaded him to grind the knife so fine that it would cut through a leather strap at a blow.

The week seemed very long to Richard. Gregory returned from the forest with good news of the little party there. Alys was becoming a capital cook and had made firm friends with m'lord. Crispin was rested and complaining less of the pain in his limbs, and as for Earl Travers, he wholeheartedly approved of Richard's plan and was in a fever of impatience that he could not lead the rescuers through the secret passage himself.

All through the week men from Sir Peter's farms came to the Manor to be armed and drilled and told, under a sacred pledge of secrecy, the plan of attack. The most dangerous moment would come when the first man came up into the chapel, for should the enemy be alerted then, they might rally around the false tombstone and prevent the rest of the men from coming out. Absolute silence would have to be observed until all were assembled in the chapel, and the men were warned to wear nothing that might jingle or clank. Rags must be tied around their feet, Sir Peter ordered, that every footfall should be as silent as a cat's. Their faces, too, must be blacked, that they might creep up on the enemy like avenging shadows out of the night. It was all so exciting that, as the days slowly passed, Richard could hardly eat, and his sleep became fitful and troubled by dreams. When at last the moment came to prepare for the march, his hands shook as he applied a mixture of soot and grease to his face, and he felt so sick and shaky that he had to keep well out of Lady Harcourt's way lest she should suspect his state of mind and, even at the eleventh hour, prevent him from going.

They set out an hour before midnight, when all light had faded from the summer sky. It was a long march to Travers Castle, but the men chosen were young and strong and would make light of a ten-mile tramp. Sir Peter alone was to ride, with Richard again behind him, and the horse's hooves

muffled with woolen rags. Sir Peter with his face blackened
and a great battle-axe thrust into his belt was a fearsome
figure, and yet comic, so that Richard had much ado not to
giggle nervously as Gregory tossed him up on to the broad
back of the weight-carrying charger. He wished he could
have had a mount of his own, but Sir Peter had not offered
him one and he had not cared to ask. Quietly the word was
given to march, and the column of men set off silently into
the darkness of the night.

Richard, jogging up and down uncomfortably behind Sir
Peter's broad back, was beset by anxiety. Suppose Odo had
been deceived and the garrison was stronger by far than
they had been led to believe? Suppose Odo was in the pay of
the enemy and had deliberately given false information?
Suppose a spy had carried news of their night attack to the
castle so that as they emerged one by one from the tunnel
they were fallen upon and killed, until there was no one left?
What would become of his father then, and little Alys? Then
a more horrible fancy still came into his mind. Suppose the
enemy knew of the tunnel and of their plans? Might they not
secure the tombstone so that it could not be opened from
below, and then, waiting until all Sir Peter's men were below
ground, suppose they made a sortie from the castle and
blocked up the entrance, entombing them all? Richard
felt sick at the thought. To be trapped underground, in the
cold, earth-smelling darkness, that would be the ultimate
horror!

As if he had read his thoughts, Sir Peter turned in the
saddle and whispered: "We must leave a strong guard at the
entrance to the passage while the rest of us go through. It
would never do to be taken in the rear."

Richard almost laughed in his relief. How could he have

been so simple as to suppose Sir Peter would endanger all his men? He was letting the darkness cast its spell of fear over him, he was not keeping his courage high.

It seemed a very long time before the column of men came to a halt and Gregory, who had been leading, came quietly to the side of Sir Peter's horse and whispered: "The entrance is just ahead, sir. So far as I can see, the undergrowth is grown up all around it. I do not think anyone has been near the spot since we escaped. Shall we go in, sir? I will lead the way."

"And I!" exclaimed Richard eagerly, but Sir Peter shook his head.

"Neither one of you," he said. "I have in mind the very man to send. He is a poacher, though he thinks I know it not, and he can walk softer than a cat and melt into the shadows as if he was a shadow himself. I shall send Jake, and behind him a small body of men who know how to use the short-sword. After them, if they report the chapel to be empty, will come the rest of us, but you, Richard, will remain at my side. I want no heroics. I desire only to deliver you alive and well to your father when he comes back to claim his own."

"May I not strike a blow for my own home?" grumbled Richard. Sir Peter smiled.

"Pick out a foe of your own size," he said gently. "No one questions your courage, Godson, but boys are no match for grown men. Now! Let us be on our way."

He dismounted from his horse, and Richard slid to the ground beside him. Then, Gregory leading the way, they went forward through the darkness to the tunnel mouth. Bushes whipped in their faces and thorns clutched at their legs, but at last they stood before what looked like a very solid outcrop of rock.

"I see no door," Sir Peter whispered, and Gregory whispered back, "Watch."

Putting both hands on the face of the stone, he pressed with all his strength. The seemingly solid rock swiveled upon a hidden iron pin, disclosing the darker mouth of a hole. A damp, earthy smell came up, and Sir Peter said anxiously: "I fear the air in the tunnel will be foul."

"Not so," said Gregory. "This tunnel was cunningly constructed, and somewhere along the way fresh air blows in. I believe there is a pipe in the roof which comes through the ground at a hidden spot."

"Jake!" whispered Sir Peter, and a small thin man with wild hair and ragged clothes came quickly out of the darkness.

"Now, master?" he asked eagerly, and at Sir Peter's nod he disappeared through the hole like a weasel into a cony's burrow. He was followed by six young men armed with broadswords and as the slight sound of their footsteps receded down the tunnel the rest of the company waited tensely for what might come.

In a very few moments a man appeared in the hole, his blackened face streaked and stained with earth and sweat.

"All is clear, master," said the man hoarsely. "Jake is in the chapel and reports there is no one about and not a sound to be heard."

A stir went through the waiting men and they pressed forward, filing silently one by one through the hole under the rock.

Richard had not meant to disobey Sir Peter, but someone pushed against him in the darkness, he staggered and caught hold of an unseen arm. Then the men pressed on, carrying him with them, and before he could recover himself he felt the dank air of the passage strike on his face. He put out his hand and touched the leather jerkin of the man in front, while from behind, someone trod hard on his heels. The blackness was absolute; it pressed down on Richard like a solid mass and he stumbled forward blindly, unable to turn back even if he had had the will.

The ground began to rise, the blackness lightened and became gray, and a rough flight of steps showed dimly ahead. Richard stumbled up them behind the leather jerkin and found himself in the familiar chapel of his home. He smelled the well-remembered smell of damp stone, and beeswax from the polished stools and altar table, and a great surge of excitement rose within him, leaving no room for fear.

The men were gathering now. Dimly he could see Jake standing by the outer door, ready to open when all were there. Gregory was near at hand, his face set and grim under its coating of soot. Suddenly Richard heard a stifled laugh, and looking around at the men, he saw white teeth gleaming in black faces as mouths opened in silent mirth.

"What is it?" he whispered, and the man to whom he spoke chuckled softly.

"The master is stuck in the entrance to the passage," he said. "Too many capons, too much sack! He has sent word we are to attack under Gregory's leadership, and you, young master, he commands to go back."

Richard hesitated. He had promised to obey his godfather, but to retreat to safety, leaving the attack to be led by a serving man, was asking much of the scion of a noble house. As he hesitated, miserably indecisive, the decision was taken out of his hands. From outside the chapel came a sudden flare of light. Someone shouted, the chapel doors were flung open, and a body of armed men rushed in.

There was no time to retreat. Richard drew the knife from his belt.

"A Travers! A Travers!" he yelled and plunged into the thick of the fight.

16

A Path of Gold

Someone was singing. It was a quiet, soothing tune like a lullaby, and perhaps it was a lullaby because through the song came a baby's voice, a little, contented coo. The two sounds blended together in Richard's head as he came slowly back to consciousness out of the dark night of pain. He lay quite still with closed eyes, wondering hazily where he was. Then a voice he knew said urgently: "M'lady! I saw his eyelids stir."

The singing stopped, he heard the rustle of skirts, and opening his eyes, he looked straight into his mother's face.

"Mother?" he said wonderingly. "How did you get here?"

"The poor child is wandering in his mind!" cried the familiar voice, and Richard, feebly turning his head, saw the face of Joanna, his nurse. Remembrance came flooding back.

He was at home! Yes, of course, they had come up into the chapel and then the enemy burst in and they had fought. But that was in the darkness and now it was daylight and he was in his mother's well-remembered bower. What had happened? Who had won? Agitatedly he tried to sit up and was pressed down on the pillows again by his mother's gentle hand.

"Who won?" he whispered, and his mother said: "The

castle is liberated, thanks be to God. Sir Peter is here with his men, and Gregory has already set out with horses and a litter to bring your father home. There, does that tell you what you want to know?"

"Am I wounded?" asked Richard, and his mother said: "You have a gash in your arm. It is not serious and will soon mend, but you lost much blood." She looked at him and tears came into her eyes. "Oh, my son, my little son, if I should have lost you!" she said. "I have missed you so much all these weary months, and they brought you to me white and still and I thought you were dead!"

"Poor Mother," said Richard. "But you have my little sister. May I see her, please?"

Joanna came to the bedside with a bundle in her arms. Out of the wrappings peeped a rosy face with bright blue eyes and a tuft of golden hair like a question mark on the top of her head. She looked at Richard solemnly and blew bubbles. Richard held out a hand and the baby clutched his little finger and held on tight.

"She is very sweet," said Richard contentedly. "Mother, has Gregory told you of Alys?"

"Indeed, yes," said Lady Travers. "The poor child!"

"You will not let her go back to her aunt and uncle to marry that horrible man?" asked Richard anxiously, and his mother looked distressed.

"That is for your father to decide," she said. "Do not trouble your head about it now, Richard. You have to regain your strength. Your poor father will be here soon and then I shall have two invalids for whom to care."

"Father does not seem like an invalid," Richard assured her. "He is just the same except that he cannot stand or walk."

"Your father is the bravest man I ever knew," said Lady Travers quietly. "To be brave in the face of danger is a splendid thing, but to be brave through months and years of pain and frustration is courage of the highest order. It is that sort of courage which your father has in full measure. He will be no less the master of us all because he is crippled, but he will need you, Richard, more urgently than a whole man needs his only son."

"I know," said Richard soberly. "I have thought a great deal about it, and I will do my best to help him."

"That is my good boy," smiled Lady Travers, and then sounds outside drew her to the window and she cried eagerly, "Here they come!"

Richard tried to rise, but he turned faint and fell back on the pillows. His mother, Joanna, and the baby all disappeared and he lay there wretchedly, his arm throbbing and his head hot and swimming. Glad cries floated up from below; he heard horses' hooves, and then his father's voice. How he longed to be down there among them all to welcome his father home! Tears came into his eyes, but he brushed them away quickly as he heard a light footfall on the stairs. The next moment the door opened, and Alys, still in her boy's gear, came eagerly into the room.

"Oh, Richard, are you badly wounded?" she cried, turning pale at the sight of his bandaged arm.

"Only a scratch," said Richard with fine carelessness.

"Did you—*kill* anyone?" whispered Alys, and Richard said: "Who knows? It was too dark to see where one struck. As the enemy rushed into the chapel, I drew my knife and—"

"Oh, hush!" Alys implored him. "I do not really want to hear."

"Girls!" said Richard scornfully. "They are all alike. If girls had their way, there would be no wars."

"And what a good thing that would be!" cried Alys. "We could all be happy then."

"No, we could not," argued Richard. "War has nothing to do with your being betrothed to the French count."

Alys's face grew anxious. "I have talked a great deal to m'lord your father about that," she said. "He has promised to see what he can do, but he says he cannot be sure of saving me because my uncle is so powerful and might come and carry me away by force. Richard, I am so worried. I thought that if only we could come here I should be safe, and now—and now—"

"It will be all right, Alys," said Richard sturdily. "I am sure it will all come right."

Joanna returned then and took Alys away to be bathed and clothed in a little green gown, which had lain in a chest ever since Lady Travers herself was a child. It was a very special gown, being richly embroidered and trimmed with fur, and had been made for Lady Travers to wear when the King visited her childhood home. She had kept it ever since in remembrance of the splendor of that day. Now Alys's fair head rose out of it, her new-washed hair, clipped by Joanna into a semblance of order, giving her a quaint look, like a mischievous page boy masquerading as a little maid.

By suppertime that night Richard was so far recovered as to insist upon being helped down to the Great Hall, where he sat by the hearth surrounded by his dogs, Mistress Stout trying hard to climb upon his knee. Opposite him lounged Sir Peter, and between them the Earl of Travers sat very erect in his own high-backed chair, his useless legs supported upon a stool and covered with a light woolen cloth.

He had had Gregory dress him in his finest clothes, with jewels glinting against rich silks and furs. He looked a splendid figure and Richard could hardly take his eyes off him, while Alys would not be persuaded to leave his side but sat on a low stool, holding one of his lean, brown, beringed hands in her own. Lady Travers too had put on her best silk robe in honor of the occasion, but her face was anxious and strained. The Earl was home again, her son was home, but as long as the war lasted, there could be no security, no peace of mind, for who could know what might come next? True, Sir Peter was there with his hundred men, but they would want to go back to their homes, and who would man the castle then? It would be left to a cripple, a twelve-year-old boy, and a few old retainers, for the knights and foot soldiers who had defended the castle during the siege were now dead or prisoners, or had escaped to fight under another baron's flag.

The Earl too was full of anxious thoughts, and while he strove to look cheerful, he could not help wondering how long they would be left to enjoy their reunion. If news of his return came to the ears of his enemies, forces might be sent to kill him, imprison his wife and children, and even raze the castle to the ground. He looked down at Alys, so trustfully clasping his hand, and almost groaned aloud. Poor child! If the Baron, her uncle, should return from a victorious campaign and ride to Travers Castle to claim her back, who would there be to defend her? No one but a cripple, a boy, and a few old men.

Supper was brought in by serving men and maids, and they were followed by the old Steward, so glad and happy that tears poured down his wrinkled face. The cooks had a wonderful feast. There was roast venison and wild duck, woodcock and pork. There was fruit from the garden and orchard and a few precious dried figs and dates which Lady Travers had been hoarding in her store cupboard for the day when Richard should come home.

Tenderly, two men lifted the Earl's chair and carried him up on to the dais, setting him down at the center of the long table. Gregory helped Richard to his place on his father's left hand, with Alys next to him. Lady Travers sat on her husband's right, with Sir Peter by her side. The hall seemed strangely empty without the company which had usually assembled there for the evening meal, and in spite of the happiness of the occasion, a sense of strain was felt by them all. Only Sir Peter ate and drank heartily and talked with Lord Travers of the chase.

It was very warm in the Great Hall. From far away in the distance came the rumble of thunder. Although it was still early evening, the sky grew black, and shadows crept into every corner of the hall. The thunder came again, louder and nearer, cracking out of the sky like a giant crushing nuts. A flash of lightning suddenly lit the world with its blinding yellow glare, then came a few heavy drops of rain, and the storm was upon them. Wind and rain assaulted the castle like enemy forces. Servants rushed to shut the outer doors, but the rain drove through the narrow windows and splattered on the stone floor. The thunder was a continual roll, and lightning turned the dark evening into a hideous, unnatural day.

Suddenly, through the storm, a sound came which was neither wind nor rain. The company at the table strained to catch the sound, apprehension gripping them all. For the sound was the sound of galloping feet. Someone was riding recklessly, furiously along the road which led to the main gates. Then, in a lull of the storm, they heard a shout, followed by the grind and rattle of the drawbridge as it spanned the moat. The drumming of hooves sounded again, hollow on the boards of the bridge, and now more people were shouting and feet were running, running to the doors of the hall.

"What is it? Oh, what is it?" cried Alys. "Have they come to fetch me back?"

The Earl sat very upright in his high-backed chair and Richard sat at his side, his eyes fixed on the door.

There came a clatter of hooves as if a horse had been reined back suddenly on its haunches. The voices were very loud now and excited. Somebody cheered, the doors were thrown open, and a man, wet to the skin and muddy past belief, rushed in, followed by a crowd of Sir Peter's men, all cheering wildly. The man came down the hall, his face alight with joy, and dropped on one knee before the Earl.

"I bring good news, m'lord!" he cried in a strong voice. "Our enemies are overthrown! Simon de Montfort is dead! The Baron Banworth is dead! Their forces are scattered, or lie dead on the battlefield of Evesham! The King is wounded, but not sorely, and has rejoined Prince Edward. England is free of the upstart foreigner. God save the King!"

"Amen to that," said Lord Travers quietly. "And God rest the soul of a man who for all his faults had something of greatness in him. Simon de Montfort was a man one might hate but could never despise. He was above the common run of men, and England will not soon forget him."

"Say you the Baron Banworth is dead?" asked Lady Travers, and the messenger nodded.

"Aye, m'lady," he said. "With my own eyes I saw him struck down."

Alys slipped out of her chair and went to Lord Travers's side.

"M'lord," she whispered. "Shall I now be free?"

He smiled. "I will petition the King to appoint me your guardian," he promised. "I do not think he will refuse."

"Peace at last," said Lady Travers softly. "It seems too good to believe."

The storm was passing over. The rain stopped, the skies lightened, the clouds parted, and a long ray of sunshine struck through the open doors and lay, like a golden path to happiness, across the Great Hall to the feet of the little company on the dais.